S.K. Das is Honorary Advisor to the Indian Space Research Organisation and the author of a number of books including *Mission Moon: Exploring the Moon with Chandrayaan 1* and *All About Rockets*.

ALL ABOUT SATELLITES

S.K. DAS

RED TURTLE

RUPA

Published in Red Turtle by
Rupa Publications India Pvt. Ltd. 2016
7/16, Ansari Road, Daryaganj
New Delhi 110002

Sales Centres:

Allahabad Bengaluru Chennai
Hyderabad Jaipur Kathmandu
Kolkata Mumbai

Copyright © S.K. Das 2016

The views and opinions expressed in this book are the author's own and the facts are as reported by him which have been verified to the extent possible, and the publishers are not in any way liable for the same.

All rights reserved.
No part of this publication may be reproduced, transmitted, or stored in a retrieval system, in any form or by any means, electronic, mechanical, photocopying, recording or otherwise, without the prior permission of the publisher.

ISBN: 978-81-291-3005-1

First impression 2016

9 7 8 8 1 2 9 1 3 0 0 5 1

The moral right of the author has been asserted.

Printed in India by Nutech Print Services, Faridabad

This book is sold subject to the condition that it shall not, by way of trade or otherwise, be lent, resold, hired out, or otherwise circulated, without the publisher's prior consent, in any form of binding or cover other than that in which it is published.

Contents

Introduction	*vii*
1. The Final Frontier	1
2. From Stone Age to Space Age	8
3. All About Orbits	17
4. Who Needs a Satellite?	33
5. What Are Satellites Made of?	67
6. 3, 2, 1...Take off!	93
7. The Life and Death of a Satellite	110
8. The Story of India's Satellite Missions	122
9. The Satellites of the Future	148
10. Experiments	151

Introduction

A metal ball, a radio, a thermometer, a battery and nitrogen gas.

Are these items for a school science project? Back in 1957, these objects captured the attention of the world. The metal ball was Sputnik 1, the first satellite to go up in space and orbit Earth. The other objects were put in Sputnik 1 to enable the satellite to function in space. For example, the radio was there to establish communication with the ground stations and broadcast radio signal pulses; the thermometer to record thermal temperature; and the battery to power the transmitters which sent signals to Earth. Sputnik 1 was filled with dry nitrogen to pressurize the satellite. History changed on 4 October 1957 when Sputnik 1 was launched by the Soviet Union, the first satellite successfully launched by man.

But what is a satellite? It is an object that moves around a planet. The moon is a satellite because it moves around Earth. The moon is a natural satellite. Many planets have satellites moving around them.

However, when we say 'satellite', we usually mean man-made satellites. These satellites are made by space scientists. These machines are launched into space, and they orbit Earth or some other body in space.

There are thousands of man-made satellites in space today. Satellites fly high in the sky, so they can see large areas of Earth at a time. Satellites have a clear view of space. That is because they fly above Earth's clouds and air. Some take pictures of Earth. Some take pictures of other planets, the sun and other planetary objects. Other satellites relay TV signals, phone calls and Internet signals around the world.

Many satellites carry cameras and scientific instruments. Satellites help scientists to study all kinds of things. They provide information about

Earth's clouds, ocean, land, water and air. They observe wildfires, volcanoes and smoke. All this information helps scientists predict weather and climate; provides information to farmers to know what crops to plant—and controls the spread of disease at the time of emergencies and disasters.

Satellites also tell us a lot about space. Some satellites watch for dangerous rays coming from the sun. Some explore stars, planets, asteroids and comets. Placed high up in space, satellites keep a constant watch over Earth and deliver a constant stream of data.

Today, more than 3,000 satellites are circling Earth. These satellites are built for a variety of missions, so each one is different. They come in all shapes and sizes. They play a variety of roles, too. For example, communication satellites link remote areas of Earth with telephone and television. Remote sensing satellites look at Earth and its oceans for changes in everything from temperature to forests, land and water. Weather satellites help in predicting the weather. Scientific satellites perform a variety of scientific missions.

Navigational satellites help aircraft and ships to navigate. Rescue satellites respond to radio distress signals. Spy satellites are up there in space, but what they do remains a secret.

Satellites have had a profound effect on our daily lives. Not a day passes without our using a communication satellite to make a long distance phone call, to use a mobile phone, or a fax machine, or even listen to the radio, watch TV and use the Internet. Satellites have touched the life of an average person more than any other technological innovation of the twentieth century.

Services from satellites in space have great potential to improve our lives on Earth. They also offer us ways of responding to the challenges of tomorrow. How we use satellites to improve our lives and meet future challenges will depend on the space scientists of tomorrow, many of whom may be from among you, the readers, who are sitting in classrooms today. This book is for you.

1
The Final Frontier

What is space?

To early man, Earth must have looked flat. During the day, they would have seen the sun rising in the east, moving slowly across the sky from east to west and disappearing in the evening. During night, they would have watched the sky peppered with twinkling dots of light and the flat disk of the moon. They would have marvelled at the sun's mysterious ability to make the journey to another world and reappear over the eastern horizon the next morning.

So, myths were born about this other world about which they knew very little. The other world, they would have thought, was the realm of the heavens where gods lived their immortal lives. But when man entered the space age and travelled through what we now call space, they found no gods. Instead, they found a strange place without air, noise or smell. It was empty and yet hostile, a world of silence and a source of very high energy.

Space: Black and Dark

Yuri Gagarin was the first man to travel into space. When he came back, he said that space looked black and dark. Why is it that the blue sky becomes black when we enter space? Since space lacks an atmosphere, there is no scattering of light. On Earth, molecules of air obstruct the passage of light. When light rays strike these molecules of air, the rays are spread or scattered in all directions. Blue light, which has the shortest wavelength, is scattered the most, and that is why the sky looks blue during the day.

Where does space begin and end?

What are the boundaries of space? Where does space begin? Where does it end? What is the difference between space and the universe?

The boundaries of space are impossible to define precisely. The universe encompasses everything that exists. Space is what lies between us and the stars, and between the stars themselves. We can say that space is the vast area of the universe outside Earth's atmosphere.

And what is atmosphere? It is the envelope of gases that covers and protects Earth. It is sustained primarily due to the effect of gravity. As we go higher and higher from Earth's surface, gravity reduces and at greater heights, the atmosphere becomes thinner and thinner. The thickness of Earth's atmosphere is really very small compared to its size. If we compare Earth to an orange, its atmosphere will be as thick as the skin of the orange.

At a height of about 200 km above our heads, a residual atmosphere is all that remains. If we go higher, the atmosphere becomes very thin and it gradually merges into space, where there is vacuum. So, we can say that the entire area above 200 km from the surface of Earth can be defined as space.

There is no upper boundary of space. Space is endless. In this vast endless space, Earth is just a tiny point, one of the planets in the sun's family. The sun is one of the 100 billion stars in the Milky Way galaxy, and there are many galaxies in the universe.

Is space empty?

Space contains such little matter that we think it is empty. For us on Earth, it is difficult to imagine such emptiness. That is because on Earth, matter is everywhere in liquid, solid or gaseous form.

Space is a vacuum. But it is also an exciting place where exchanges of energy take place. Such exchange happens by radiation. Also, the vacuum of space is not absolute because space contains atoms, dust and solid debris of all kinds.

There are more than 16,000 objects larger than 10 cm in space, produced by human activities. These objects include 3,100 operating satellites, 1,600 launch vehicle stages and over 9,300 objects of debris. The number of objects between 1 and 10 cm is estimated to be at 2,00,000, and the number of objects smaller than 1 cm, at several million.

Is space hot or cold?

There is no simple answer. Without the sun, Earth and other stars, the temperature in space would be extremely low; in fact, as low as –270 degree Centigrade! Significant temperature variations between objects in space, and between two sides of the same object, occur due to the stars that are sources of heat. In the vacuum of space, only radiation allows heat to propagate. As a result, the temperature differences can be high. For example, at an altitude of 400 km, the temperature can drop from +120 degree Centigrade to –150 degree Centigrade in a matter of minutes.

What is space really like?

When you look up at the stars in the night sky, does space seem like a peaceful, quiet sort of place? It is not. Space environment is harsh, hazardous and violent. In fact, Earth's atmosphere, ozone layer and magnetic field act as a shield protecting us from the harsh conditions of the space environment which is much more hostile than we can imagine. The atmosphere acts as a blanket and keeps Earth warm and comfortable through the greenhouse effect. The Earth's magnetic field also protects us from many hazards of the space environment.

DID YOU KNOW?

1. In space, there is no night and no day.
2. On Earth, the atmosphere gives the sky its blue colour. In space, there is no atmosphere so it remains in perpetual darkness.
3. There is no sound in space, either. Sound vibrations can travel only in a medium. In the vacuum of space, there is no medium, and therefore, no sound.

So what is really going on out there?

Out there in space, the sun is constantly shedding a stream of particles and radiation called the solar wind, which could kill human beings. Every year, massive outbursts of energy, called solar flares, are hurled into space at speeds of up to 50,000 km per hour. Closer to Earth, the solar wind combines with the flux of particles ejected by star outbursts to form cosmic radiation. These particles form the Van Allen radiation belts.

In space there are meteoroids, which are small particles in interplanetary space. Even though the size of these particles are small (one millimetre in diameter), their impact can cause damage to satellite components due to their high velocities. These particles travel at a velocity of 20 to 70 km per second.

The satellites we send into space are exposed to extreme hot and cold temperatures; and hazard from high-energy radioactive particles. Despite this harsh and hostile environment, satellites have to work with very high reliability throughout their long life.

2
From Stone Age to Space Age

Who says the world is flat?

For a long time, people believed that Earth was a flat body surrounded by oceans and lay at the centre of the universe. It was only in the third century BC that some Greek astronomers deduced that the sun is in the centre and Earth and other planets orbit around it. Other Greeks did not accept this explanation. Ptolemachs, the renowned Greek scholar, still believed that Earth was at the centre of the universe, and that is why this theory is known as the Ptolemaic or the geocentric system of the world.

The Christian church supported the geocentric view of the world. The Church even turned it into a dogma and punished people who dared to oppose it. It was only in 1543 AD, almost eighteen centuries after the Greeks talked about it, that Copernicus gave scientific proof of a solar system with the sun at its centre. Although this discovery was path-breaking, Copernicus was afraid to publish his book when he was alive, because he feared he would suffer at the hands of the Church. When the book was finally published after his death, the Church banned the book.

The great Indian astronomer, Aryabhata, who lived in the fifth century AD, proposed a model in which Earth turns on its own axis. His calculations were based on the heliocentric model, in which planets orbit the sun. It was to recognize his great contribution to astronomy that India's first satellite was called Aryabhata.

What makes the planets move?

At the beginning of the seventeenth century, Johannes Kepler, a German astronomer, gave the first scientific explanation of planetary motion. He told us how planets moved, but he did not tell us why. It was Isaac Newton who discovered why the planets moved the way they did. This was because of universal gravitation. Isaac Newton was a great scientist who lived more than 300 years ago. He wrote about many of the laws of motion that we see at work every day.

To explain how one body can orbit another, imagine a cannon on top of a very tall mountain, Newton said.

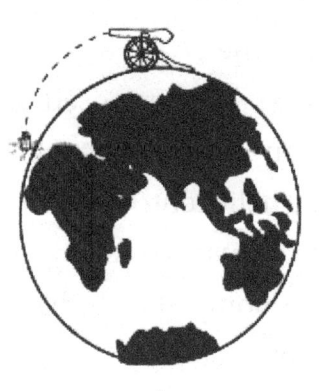
A

The cannon is loaded with gunpowder and fired. The cannonball follows a curve faster and faster as a result of Earth's gravity, and hits Earth some distance away (Picture A).

What if we use more gunpowder? The cannonball moves faster and goes farther before gravity pulls it back to Earth (Picture B).

If we use even more gunpowder, the cannonball goes so fast that it goes all the way around the world. It becomes a satellite of Earth. If we use enough gunpowder, the cannon ball will go so fast that it will completely escape Earth's gravity and head out into space (Picture C).

B

C

That is how the idea of a satellite was born.

In 1903, Konstantin Tsiolkovsky published his book *The Exploration of Cosmic Space by Means of Reaction Devices*, which showed mathematically how a satellite could be launched to achieve Earth orbit. Tsiolkovsky calculated the speed required to orbit around Earth at 8 km per second and a rocket fuelled by liquid hydrogen and liquid oxygen could achieve this. In 1928, Herman Potočnik wrote a book, *The Problem of Space Travel*, describing the use of a satellite for detailed observation of Earth and how the special condition of space could be useful for scientific experiments.

Who won the satellite race?

The Soviet Union launched Sputnik 1, the world's first satellite, on 4 October 1957. Though it was a small satellite and took about 98 minutes to orbit Earth, its successful launch was a historic event. It was not only mankind's first satellite but also the first time in human history when a rocket had cleared Earth's gravity and put a satellite into orbit. That is why 4 October 1957 is regarded as the beginning of the Space Age.

Sputnik 1 was a small and simple satellite. It was a 58 cm-83 kg metal ball and its contents were meagre by today's standards. All it contained were a thermometer, two thermostat switches, two batteries, a radio transmitter with long antennae and nitrogen gas. It is a good example of just how simple a satellite can be. Today's satellites are far more complex but the basic idea is the same. Though the launch of Sputnik 1 changed history, no photographs were taken of this famous launch because of the great political secrecy prevailing in the Soviet Union at that time.

Transmissions from Sputnik 1 died along with its batteries after three weeks of its launch. After 92 days, gravity took over and Sputnik 1 burned in Earth's atmosphere.

Dog days in space

In 1957, Soviet Union stunned the world with a new space sensation — the launch of Sputnik 2 carrying a passenger on board. Sputnik 2 weighed 508 kg — more than six times the weight of Sputnik 1. There was a cabin inside Sputnik 2 housing the world's first space passenger, the mongrel dog Laika.

The core of Sputnik 2 was the dog cabin, measuring 0.8 m in length and 0.64 m in diameter. The aluminium cabin was equipped with sensors to measure cabin pressure and temperature as well as the canine passenger's blood pressure, breath frequency and heartbeat. These instruments allowed scientists on the ground to monitor what happened to the dog in space.

The launch vehicle carrying Sputnik 2 lifted off at dawn on 3 November 1957. As reports later revealed, Laika's heart was beating 260 cycles per minute, or three times higher than normal during the ride to the orbit. The frequency of her breathing also rose 4-5 times above usual. However, the dog survived the launch unscathed. Laika survived in orbit for four days but died when the cabin overheated.

Sputnik 2 stayed in orbit for almost 200 days. It carried a number of research instruments, making it the world's first space laboratory.

The Americans Join the Race

When the Soviet Union launched Sputnik 1 and Sputnik 2 in quick succession, there was a great deal of resentment in the United States as the Americans felt they were getting left behind. In December 1957, the date for the launch of the Vanguard satellite was set. But it turned out to be a disaster. When the rocket was launched, it rose three feet into the air, shook violently and disintegrated into flames.

However, the next launch of an American satellite, Explorer 1 on 31 January 1958, was successful. The satellite weighed only 14 kg. It was certainly smaller than both Sputnik 1 and Sputnik 2, but it made an important discovery. It detected the Van Allen radiation belts.

Van Allen Radiation Belts

These are radiation belts encircling Earth.

They contain charged particles such as protons and electrons which are permanently trapped in the Earth's magnetic field. These belts were detected by a small instrument to measure radiation which had been put aboard the Explorer 1 by the physicist James Van Allen. That is why these belts are called the Van Allen radiation belts. The trapped particles in these belts are a threat to the sensitive components of satellites and a serious hazard for manned flights.

The launch of Sputnik 1, therefore, started off an aggressive international space programme. An enormous infrastructure of space research, industrial activities and university programmes came into being following the launch of the first satellites, eventually leading to the development of more and more sophisticated satellite technology.

3
All About Orbits

In science fiction movies, we see a spacecraft going wherever it wants to go. But it's not like that in real life. A satellite moves in space in a fixed path called an orbit (a spacecraft becomes a satellite once it is in orbit). Every satellite has an orbital path and the type of path it takes depends on its velocity and direction. The orbit of a satellite is governed by various laws of physics. A satellite's orbit is decided depending on the mission that it has to carry out.

What holds a satellite in its orbit?

A satellite stays in its orbit due to the balance

between two forces. One force is the centrifugal force caused due to the satellite moving around Earth. The other is Earth's gravitational pull.

The orbit of a satellite depends on the balance between these two forces. The orbit is a combination of the satellite's velocity (the speed at which it travels in a straight line) and the force of Earth's gravitational pull on the satellite. The gravitational pull is the result of the mass or weight of Earth and the mass of the satellite. The force of gravity prevents the satellite from flying

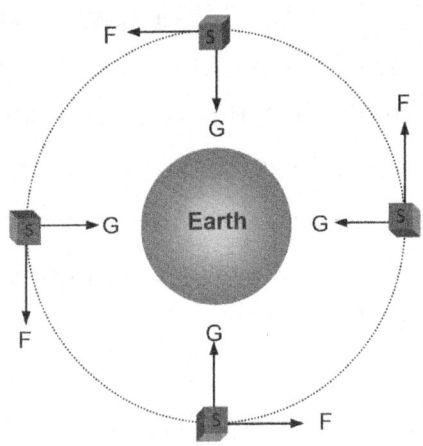

S - Satellite;   G - Gravitational Pull;   F - Forward Motion

Forces Acting on a Satellite

out in a straight line away from Earth, and the satellite's velocity prevents the force of gravity from pulling the satellite back to Earth.

How is an orbit chosen

Why should we have a satellite in one particular orbit and not in another? When scientists design a satellite, they choose an orbit that is appropriate to its functions. The orbit depends on the satellite's inclination and the mean distance from the planet. The inclination is the angle at which the satellite is tilted with reference to Earth's equator.

The functions of the satellite decide the orbit in which it should be placed. For example, a satellite which is in an orbit high up in space will not be able to see objects on Earth in as much detail as satellites that are in orbits lower and closer to Earth's surface. Factors such as the speed at which the satellite is moving in the orbit, the angle over Earth that the satellite takes, the areas which the satellite can see, and the frequency with which the satellite passes over the same portions of Earth are important considerations while choosing an orbit.

The satellite can be made to move in a new orbit by firing small rockets (thrusters) located in a satellite, in the desired direction. The speed of the satellite can also be increased or decreased by this method and the orbital height or inclination can also be changed.

What are Kepler's Laws of Planetary Motion

When people first discovered that planets orbited around the sun, they thought that orbits should be in the shape of a circle. It was not till 1601 that Johannes Kepler, using precise measurements taken by the astronomer Tycho Brahe, determined that the planets actually orbit in ellipses around the sun. An ellipse looks like a circle that has been slightly squashed. It is like an oval, or an egg.

Orbits follow some rules that are mentioned in Kepler's Laws of Planetary Motion.

Kepler's Laws

1. The orbit of every planet is an ellipse with the sun at one focus of the ellipse.
2. A line joining a planet and the sun sweeps out equal areas during equal intervals of time.
3. The square of the time taken for a planet to complete one revolution around the sun is directly proportional to the cube of its mean distance from the sun.

Kepler's Laws hold good for the satellites moving around Earth, Moon, Mars and other bodies in space.

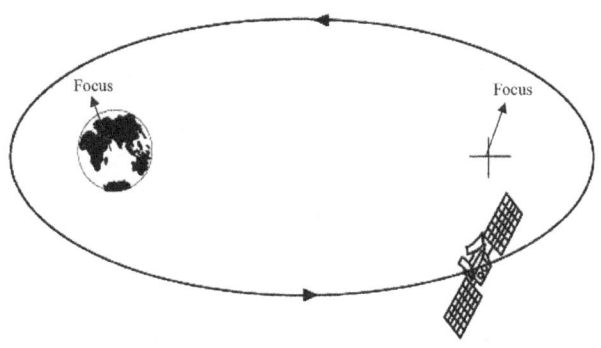

Kepler's First Law

As per Kepler's First Law, the satellite moves around Earth in an elliptical orbit as shown in the picture above. Observe that an elliptical orbit has two foci and Earth is at one of them. If no other forces are acting on the satellite, either by orbit control or by gravity forces from other bodies, the satellite will move in this orbit forever.

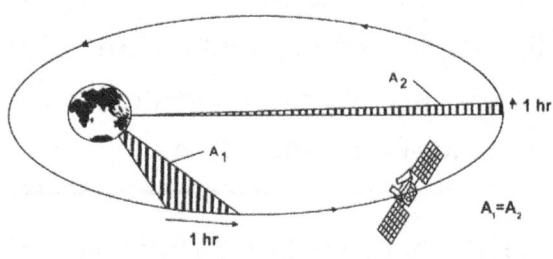

Kepler's Second Law

In the diagram above, the shaded area A1 is the area swept out by the orbiting satellite in a one-hour time period at a location near Earth and A2 is the area swept out by the satellite in a one-hour period around the point farthest from Earth. According to Kepler, A2 is equal to A1. This means the satellite moves much faster at locations near Earth and slows down as it approaches the point farthest from Earth.

After discovering these two laws, Kepler went on to measure the 'eccentricity' of orbits. Eccentricity is a measure of how circular a satellite's orbit is. For a perfectly circular orbit, the eccentricity is zero. Elliptical orbits have eccentricities between zero and one.

Kepler's Third Law compares the orbital period and radius of orbit of a planet to those of other planets. Unlike Kepler's first and second laws that describe the motion of a single planet, the Third Law makes a comparison between the motions of different planets.

DID YOU KNOW?

There are six orbital parameters that help us to understand the shape and size of the orbit, but we need to know the three important parameters. They are:
Apogee, or the maximum distance from Earth.
Perigee, or the minimum distance from Earth.
(For the orbits of planets around the sun, the terms used are **perihelion** for shortest distance from the sun, and **aphelion** for the farthest distance from the sun.)
The **inclination** is the angle between the orbital plane and Earth's equatorial plane.

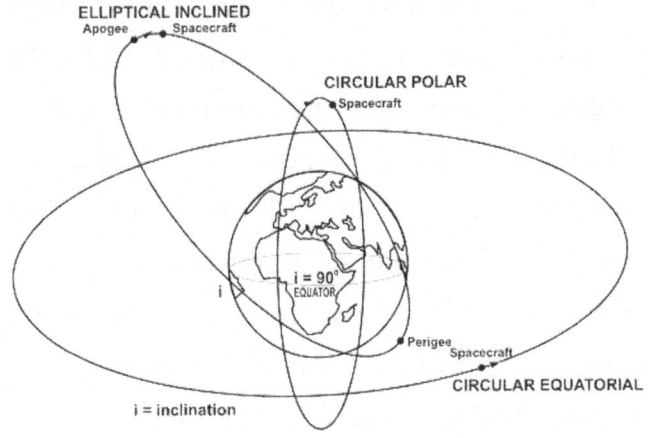

Orbital Parameters

A satellite that is in an orbit with some inclined angle is in an **inclined orbit**.

A satellite that is in orbit in the equatorial plane (inclination angle = 0 degree) is in an **equatorial orbit**.

A satellite that has an inclination angle of near 90 degrees is in a **polar orbit**.

What are the orbits in common use?

If a satellite designer uses all possible combinations of orbit parameters, the number of orbits formed can be innumerable. But experience has narrowed down the list of orbits only to a few that are in common use.

Geostationary Orbit

The geostationary orbit (GSO) is a circular orbit at 35,786 km right above the equator of Earth. In this orbit, the time taken for a satellite to orbit around Earth is approximately 24 hours (called one sidereal day). The satellite looks stationary from any point on Earth. It is ideally suited for the transfer of communication signals between

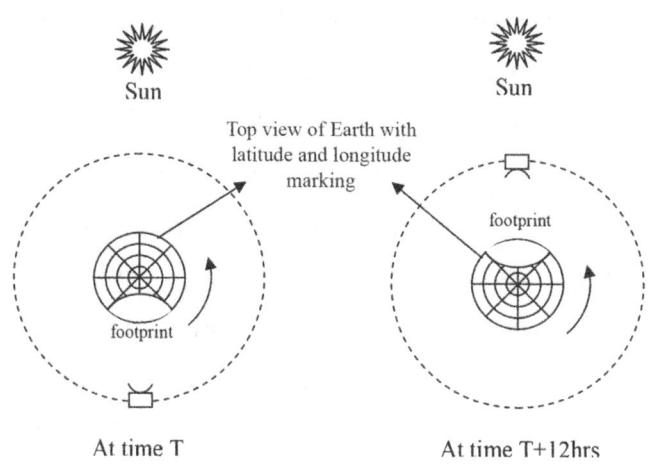

Geostationary Orbit

two or more points on Earth through a relay that is fixed in a satellite. When a satellite is in the GSO, its instruments look at a certain area of Earth. That area of Earth is called the footprint of the satellite.

In 1945, Arthur C. Clarke, a British scientist who wrote science fiction, had an idea that seemed quite odd at that time. The idea was that, if we put a radio relay tower in the sky in the form of a satellite, we can use it to transmit signals over great distances. At the time Clarke put forward his idea, transmissions were made by microwave relay systems. What it meant was that relay towers had to be put on hilltops every 48 km or so. These relay towers picked up signals and re-transmitted them at the correct angle. There was a big problem with this system. It could work only on land. The system did not work over large bodies of water. Clarke's suggestion was that a satellite positioned at 36,000 km or more above Earth could transmit signals over far greater distances than the existing system. More importantly, it could transmit them over large bodies of water like seas or oceans. Clarke said that only three satellites put in this orbit above Earth could provide telecommunication services throughout the world.

Why is this orbit called geostationary? It is because a satellite in this orbit appears to remain in the same spot in the sky all the time. In reality, the satellite is travelling at almost the same speed as Earth is rotating below it, but it looks as if it stays still regardless of the direction in which it travels, east or west. The period of revolution for the GSO is 23 hours and 56 minutes, which is almost the same time taken by Earth to complete one rotation about its axis. It is four minutes shorter than the 24-hour mean solar day because of Earth's movement around the sun.

The satellites placed above the GSO take more than 24 hours to complete one revolution and hence they seem to be lagging from a point on

Earth. Similarly, satellites placed below the GSO take less than 24 hours to complete one revolution and they seem to be leading with time. Therefore there is only one GSO.

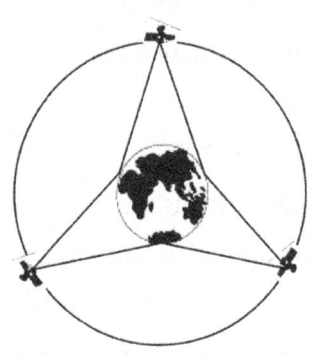

Getting continuous global communication services with three satellites

A satellite in the geostationary orbit can keep radio contact with all the ground stations located on about one-third of Earth. Thus only three communication satellites placed 120 degrees apart from each other in the GSO can provide continuous global communication services.

Though three satellites can provide coverage over the entire earth, the demand for satellite bandwidth cannot be met by just three satellites. Hence, many countries have placed their satellites in the GSO. Around 3,000 communication satellites are now placed in this orbit. The number of satellites that can operate in GSO is limited. There should be some distance between the satellites operating in this orbit so that they do not interfere with each other. That is why international treaties allot countries locations in the GSO (called orbital slots) to operate their satellites, ensuring the minimum distance is in place.

Low Earth Orbit

The low earth orbit (LEO) ranges from 200 to 2,000 km. A satellite in the LEO travels at around 27,000 km per hour and makes one revolution of Earth every 90 to 100 minutes. It can observe Earth very well because the altitude

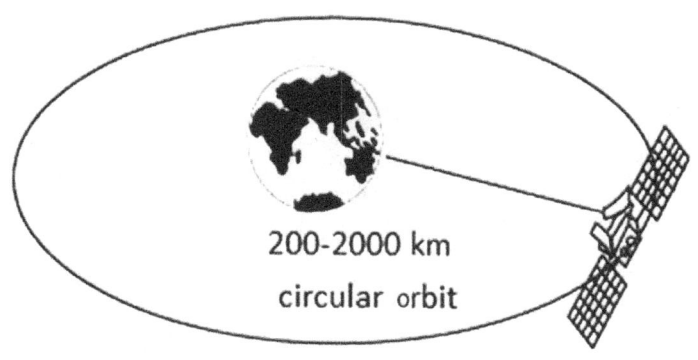

Low Earth Orbit

is not high. One advantage of a LEO satellite is that it can see clouds and weather patterns on Earth from the outside. Since it flies very close to Earth's atmosphere, it is particularly useful for atmospheric studies.

Medium Earth Orbit

The range from 10,000 to 20,000 km is referred to as the medium earth orbit (MEO). It is located between the LEO and the GSO orbit. This orbit is generally used for meteorological purposes, remote sensing and by position location applications (navigation).

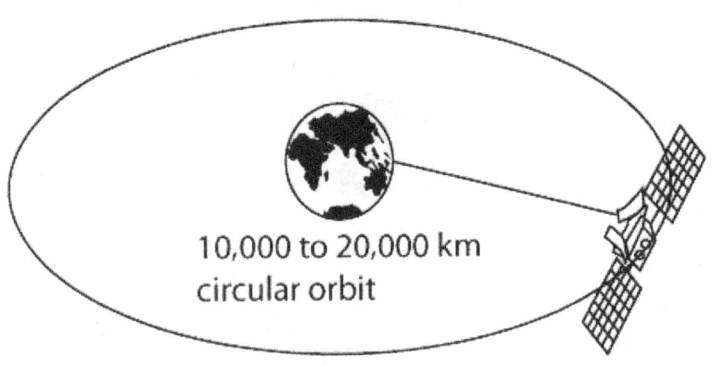

Medium Earth Orbit

Polar Orbit

A circular orbit with an inclination of about 90 degrees to the equator is called polar orbit. It is called polar orbit because when a satellite in this orbit goes around Earth, it passes over both the north and south poles. As Earth rotates to the east underneath the satellite, which is travelling north and south, it can cover the entire surface of Earth. Polar orbits are usually medium or low orbits. The satellites placed in low earth polar orbits are at an altitude of 600 km make and about 15 to 16 revolutions around Earth in a day.

Polar Orbit

Sun-synchronous Orbit

Sun-synchronous orbit is a special type of polar orbit. Like in the polar orbit, a satellite in the sun-synchronous orbit travels from the north to the south pole as Earth turns below it. But there is a difference. In a sun-synchronous orbit, the satellite passes over the same part of Earth roughly at the same local time each day. This ensures uniformity of sunlight intensity over the part of Earth being imaged.

Equatorial Orbit

The orbit that is along the line of Earth's equator is called equatorial orbit. A satellite in the equatorial orbit flies along the line of Earth's equator. To get into the equatorial orbit, a satellite must be launched from a place on Earth that is close to the equator. Equatorial orbits are usually medium, low or geostationary orbits.

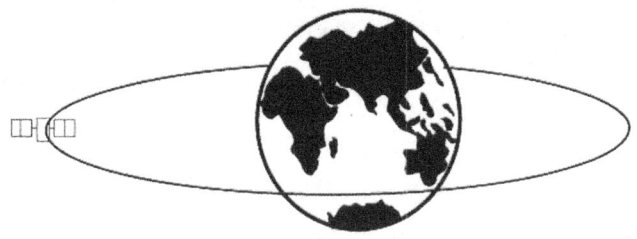

Equatorial Orbit

4
Who Needs a Satellite?

Are there many kinds of satellites?

Satellites are launched to do specific jobs. The type of satellite that is launched to monitor cloud patterns for a weather station is different from a satellite launched to send television signals. Here are some satellites that are commonly used:

Communication Satellites

Communication satellites allow radio, television and telephone transmissions to be sent live anywhere in the world. They use electromagnetic waves to convey signals.

Communication satellites play two kinds of role in communication: passive and active. They play a passive role when they are used to bounce signals from Earth back to another location on Earth. They play an active role when they carry electronic devices called transponders for receiving, amplifying and re-transmitting signals to Earth.

The transponder is a radio device that receives the signals at one frequency and then amplifies it and re-transmits it back to Earth on another frequency. A communication satellite contains a large number of transponders. Antennae in the ground station located on Earth are used to transmit and receive signals. The antennae are pointed very precisely at the satellite.

Communication satellites work through radio waves or microwaves. Microwave communication on land is essentially line-of-sight communication. What it means is that communication is possible only when two microwave stations (towers) are in line and they can see one another. Communication satellites also work in line-of-sight mode.

Microwave

Microwave is a form of electromagnetic radiation that is beyond the range of visible light spectrum in the wavelength scale. Microwaves have very high frequencies with wavelengths of 1 mm to 50 cm.

DID YOU KNOW?

- Ground stations are the **ground segment** of a satellite communication system while the satellite is the **space segment**.
- The transmission system from the ground station to satellite is called an **uplink**, and from the satellite to Earth is called a **downlink**.
- Voice, video and data are converted into electronic signals which can be sent from one gadget (e.g. TV, Radio, Computer, Tablet, Smartphone etc.) to another. Such signals are called **baseband signals**.
- The baseband signals cannot be sent directly to satellites as they are weak and prone to getting distorted. Hence the baseband signals are translated into microwave frequencies which act as **carriers**.

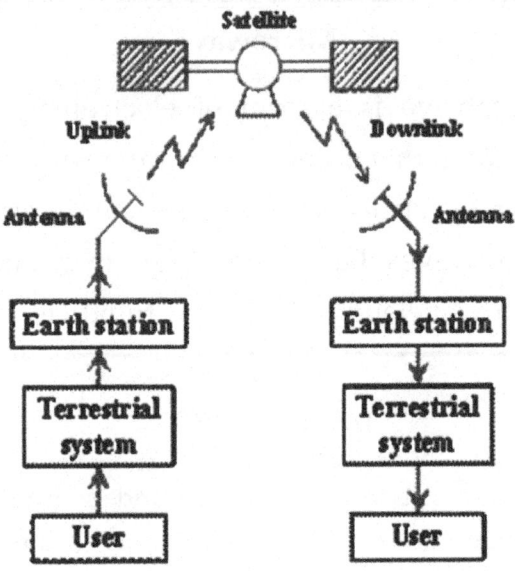

- An uplink system translates baseband signals to microwave carriers and sends them to the satellite. The satellite receives the uplink carrier(s) and relays it back to Earth in another microwave carrier. The receive systems pick up the downlink carrier(s) and converts it back to baseband signals.

Before we had communication satellites, radio or telephone transmissions could not be made over long distances. This was because these signals travel in straight lines and they cannot bend round Earth to reach a destination far away. Once satellites were invented, these signals could be sent into space and then directly to their destination.

There is a class of satellite communication system known as the Direct Broadcast Satellite (DBS) system. This system offers direct broadcast service for radio and television. Direct-to-Home (DTH) satellites belong to the DBS system. These are high-power satellites used only for providing television broadcasting. Using a small dish antenna on the terrace of a house, TV signals from a DTH satellite can be received at home. High-power communication satellites are also used for providing feeder signals to cable television services.

Similar to DTH satellites, many countries have launched high throughput satellites (HTS) which provide Internet service to homes directly. The customer-end systems of internet users are similar to DTH systems, with a small dish and a set-top box. Instead of the TV, computers are connected to the set-top box. HTS satellites are helpful in providing Internet to people living in different geographical regions, even far-flung areas.

Remote Sensing Satellites

Remote sensing is a way of gathering information about an object or area without actually touching it. It is like our eyes, ears and skin (sensors) giving us remotely sensed information about the size, colour, location and temperature of an object. We do not have to touch a heater to tell if it is hot or not. From several inches away, the nerve endings in our fingers can discern whether the heater is on, thus remotely sensing its status.

Remote sensing satellites observe and measure Earth's environment from space. They are usually put into space to monitor resources important for human beings. This can be done best from space because a satellite in orbit can take photographs of large expanses of land and water. Since these satellites are able to take photographs and observe areas all over the globe, they can monitor areas in which the climate is very harsh or which are very difficult to reach by land.

How does a remote sensing satellite work? From its orbit, the satellite detects radiation (e.g. light, temperature) that is reflected/scattered or emitted by different objects on Earth. Every object emits electromagnetic radiation in different wavelengths by virtue of its existence (temperature, light and sound are special cases of electromagnetic radiation). By measuring such radiation the satellite identifies a number of features on land like vegetation, water, soil, snow etc. through their spectral signatures. What are spectral signatures? The definition comes later on p. 43. Such information is very useful in planning and developmental activities and also in natural resource management.

Remote sensing is achieved in two ways. One is passive remote sensing, in which satellites capture the electromagnetic radiation emitted by different objects on the surface of Earth. A variety of cameras with different capabilities — including infrared cameras — are used to capture images. The second type is active remote sensing, in which satellites send microwave radiation towards Earth and measure the reflected radiation. Radars operating at different frequency bands are used in microwave remote sensing. The advantage of microwave radiation is that it can pass through all types of clouds and therefore can be used in all weather conditions. So, unlike cameras, radars can be used at night and on cloudy days. India has launched both types of remote sensing satellites.

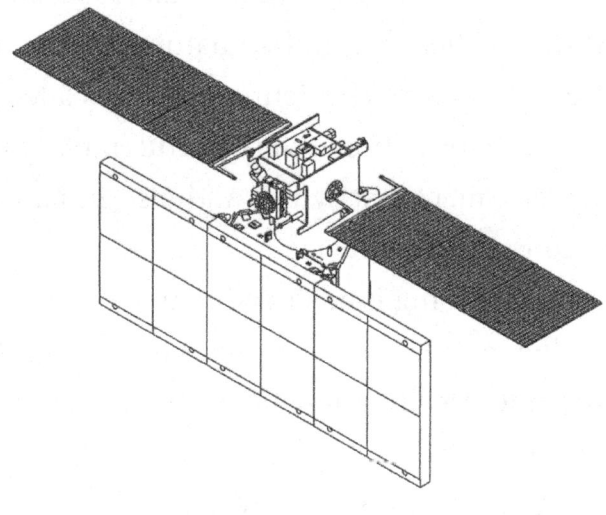

Risat-1

Remote Sensing Applications

- Remote sensing satellites view the same object in many different ways: as a photographic

image which records what our eyes can see; as a thermal image showing activities that transmit heat; and through radar that can captures a terrain even through cloud cover and at night.
- They record information in 'real time'; that is, as an event is happening.
- They document changes in events at regular intervals, recording the long-term effects of deforestation or volcanic eruptions.

Data from remote sensing satellites is used for several things. It is used for mapping land and water resources. For example, it can be used to locate groundwater and prepare groundwater maps for the entire country. Using these maps, sites can be located for drilling wells in villages that have acute shortage of drinking water. It can also be used for mapping forests and wastelands, to search for minerals and petroleum deposits, to plot ancient riverbeds in the desert, to identify cyclone, flood and earthquake-prone areas and to search for shipwrecks on the ocean floor.

Remote sensing satellites can identify whether a field is planted with rice, wheat or maize by reading each crop's spectral signature (the wavelength of light each kind of plant reflects back into the atmosphere). Scientists can also observe some amazing things about crops from a satellite image taken from a few hundred kilometres away. They can say whether the crop has just been planted or if it is ready for harvesting, if it is suffering from a disease or is being attacked by pests. This kind of information is very helpful to farmers as well as to governments for planning and management activities.

Estimating Crop Yields

Remote sensing is also used to estimate crop yields. For example, data from its remote sensing satellite has enabled ISRO to predict the yield from crops a month in advance of harvest to a level of accuracy that is as high as 90 per cent.

Remote sensing satellites are generally launched in the polar circular sun-synchronous orbit at a height of 900 km, so that they always cross the equator at a constant local solar time. These satellites are earth-facing satellites: their cameras or imaging devices always face Earth.

Weather Satellites

Let us first understand the difference between weather and climate. **Weather** consists of short-term changes (minutes to months) in atmospheric parameters like temperature, humidity, rainfall, cloudiness, sunshine, visibility and wind. Weather can change from minutes to seasonal time scales. When we talk about weather, we say things like 'it is very hot today and there is likelihood of thunderstorm in the evening,' or 'it is a rainy day,' etc. **Climate** is the average of weather over time and space (long-term patterns of weather in a particular area). For example, we receive monsoon rains during June to September, and we call it the monsoon climate. On the whole, climate is what we expect (for example, timely onset of monsoon with good rains), and weather is what we get (for example, the delayed onset of monsoon with dry spell).

When we watch a TV news channel, we see weather bulletins with satellite images showing the advance of weather fronts. These images are from weather satellites.

DID YOU KNOW?

A network of weather satellites orbit Earth to provide real-time monitoring of our environment. Apart from providing material for making weather predictions, these satellites give us very important information about our environment.

Weather satellites measure radiation from Earth's surface and atmosphere, and tell us about the amounts of heat and energy being released from Earth and its atmosphere.

They give fishermen valuable information about the temperature of the sea.

They monitor the amount of snow in winter, the movement of ice fields in the Arctic and Antarctic and the depth of the ocean.

Some weather satellites have a water vapour sensor that can measure and describe how much water vapour there is in different parts of the atmosphere. They detect volcanic eruptions and the motion of ash clouds.

These satellites also get information from data collection platforms located on the surface of Earth. These include transmitters floating in the sea (buoys), gauges recording levels of water in rivers, balloons, automated weather stations, stations that measure earthquakes and tidal wave conditions and from ships. This information, sent to the satellite from the ground, is then relayed from the satellite to a central receiving station back on Earth.

There are two types of weather satellites: those in the GSO and those in the polar orbit. The geostationary weather satellites, orbiting at a height of 35,786 km, monitor and measure the same region of Earth all the time. But they usually measure this in real time, by sending photographs to the ground stations as soon as the camera takes the picture. A series of photographs are then displayed in sequence in the form of a movie showing the movement of clouds. This allows weather forecasters to watch the progress of large weather systems such as fronts, storms and hurricanes. Forecasters can also find out the wind direction and speed by monitoring cloud movement.

The other type of weather satellites is in the polar orbit. These satellites pass over the north and south poles once in each revolution. As Earth rotates to the east beneath the satellite, each pass of the satellite monitors a narrow area running from north to south, to the west of the previous pass. These strips are then pieced together to produce a picture of a larger area. Polar satellites orbit at a height of about 850 km. This means that the polar weather satellites can photograph clouds from closer than the geostationary weather satellites do. Polar satellites, therefore, provide more detailed information about violent storms and cloud systems.

The first weather satellite in the world was TIROS-1, launched by the United States in

1960. It was in a circular orbit at an altitude of 1,000 km. TIROS-1 had television cameras that took thousands of cloud pictures. Looking at these cloud pictures, weather scientists had the opportunity, for the first time, to get a clear idea of weather conditions over a large area of Earth. Scientists were also able to identify and track cyclonic storms over the oceans from the characteristic shapes of the clouds. This was very useful since cyclonic storms cause great deal of damage to life and property.

Navigation Satellites

Satellites for navigation were developed because ships needed to know exactly where they were at any given time. The idea of navigation is to determine position (latitude, longitude and altitude) of a fixed or moving platform on Earth. In the past, navigation was done on the basis of astronomical observations, the magnetic compass, radio navigation and the gyrocompass. Satellite navigation, however, is the most accurate method.

A person or a vehicle carrying a navigation receiver determines its position by measuring its distance from navigation satellites. This means that we can figure out exactly where a satellite is in space and exactly how far we are from it. The navigation satellites send their precise orbital positions in space and accurate time regularly. Such signals sent by navigation satellites are called navigation messages and they are in the international standard format. The receivers, generally called Global Positioning Systems (GPS), receive navigation messages and determine their precise position with an accuracy of a few meters. Marking receiver positions on the map has a variety of applications, like vehicular navigation, fleet monitoring, survey of forests, canals, etc.

The precise distance to the satellite is calculated using the time taken by the signal to travel from the satellite to the receiver. It may be noted that navigation signals from satellites are a form of electromagnetic radiation that travel at the speed of light i.e. 297,600 km per second. Navigation satellites carry very precise clocks (atomic clocks) which help in determining accurate time, distance and position.

We need at least four satellites to know the position. Once distance from these four satellites is known, position in three dimensions (latitude, longitude and altitude) can be calculated by the triangulation technique, and velocity in three dimensions can be computed by shifts in the received signal.

The Transit

The US Navy launched the first navigation system in the world, called TRANSIT, consisting of five satellites. A number of ground stations on Earth regularly determined the orbit position of these satellites and this information was fed into the tape recorders of the satellites twice a day. These satellites were used for the navigation of the nuclear submarine *Polaris* and the ships of the US Navy. This was very useful for the military because neither the submarine nor the ships transmitted any radio signal, and the enemy could not detect their actual position.

Navigation satellites now provide very accurate information about position, velocity and time to ships and aircraft. The best-known satellite navigation system in the world is the GPS of the United States. There are thirty satellites in this system, which are placed in a circular orbit at a height of 20,200 km. Five ground stations on Earth regularly track these satellites to provide navigational information to these satellites. To locate a position on Earth, a specially made GPS receiver with an in-built computer is used which tracks the GPS satellites and calculates the position in a few minutes. GPS gives an accuracy of upto a few centimetres.

How does GPS work? Let us assume that a person is lost and wants to find out where exactly he is. Let us say that the person discovers that he is at 18,000 km from Satellite A. So, the person knows that he is somewhere in the universe on an imaginary sphere that has a radius of 18,000 km with the satellite in the exact middle.

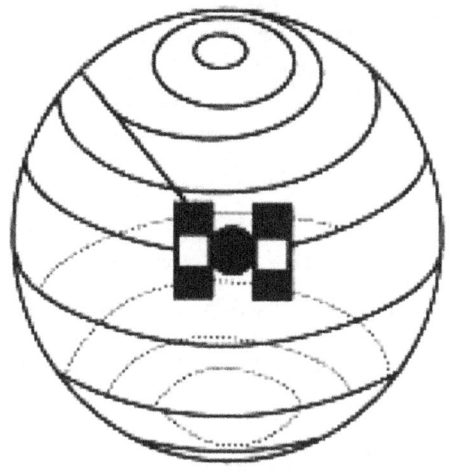

Person must be somewhere on sphere that is
18,000 km from Satellite A

If the person also knows that he is 19,000 km from another satellite (Satellite B), it narrows down the location of the person even more. Now, the only place in the universe where a person can be 18,000 km from Satellite A and 19,000 km from Satellite B is on the circle where these two spheres intersect.

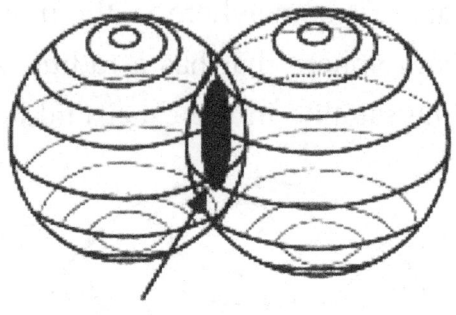

Person must be somewhere in the circle where the two spheres overlap

If, at the same time, the person is 20,000 km from a Satellite C, there are only two points in space where that can be true. Those two points are where the 20,000 km sphere cuts through the circle that is the intersection of the 18,000 km sphere and the 19,000 km sphere.

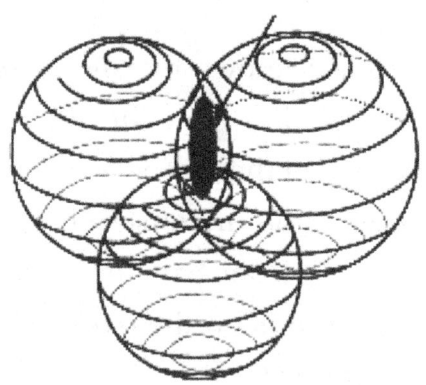

Now there are only two points where the person can be located

A fourth measurement is made from another satellite, but usually, three measurements are sufficient. This is the basic principle behind GPS. Satellites are used as reference points to triangulate a position somewhere on Earth. The rest of the system is used to make the process more accurate and easier.

A Navigation Receiver in the Car

Cars now have special GPS receivers with in-built computers for the purpose of navigation. The GPS receiver tracks the satellites and determines the location of the car in terms of latitude and longitude. The navigation system applies this location to the map stored in the memory of the computer and calculates a route to the destination entered in the computer. As the driver drives on the selected route, the system continuously provides guidance by showing the route on the screen of the computer. The navigation system provides visual and audio instructions so that the driver does not have to take his eyes off the road.

The navigation system also gives other useful tips such as the locations of petrol stations, eating joints, hospitals etc. on the way.

Russia has a global satellite navigation system called GLONASS which consists of twenty-four satellites in a circular orbit at a height of 19,100 km. India is developing a satellite navigation system (IRNSS) consisting of seven satellites. Europe's satellite navigation project, called Galileo, will have thirty satellites. China and Japan are also developing navigation satellites.

Search and Rescue Satellites

We have seen how satellites can transmit radio and television signals. But can they save lives too? Yes! Search and rescue satellites are designed to provide a way for ships at sea and aircraft to communicate from remote areas, and thereby, save lives of people affected by natural disasters or other emergencies. In all such cases, the chances of survival depend on the immediate identification of the location of the disaster area in order to start rescue operations.

Search and rescue satellites can detect and locate emergency beacons carried by ships and aircraft in remote and inaccessible places. Using mathematical calculations involving the Doppler effect, scientists can calculate the signal into coordinates, and determine the location of the distress signal within four kilometres. Modern emergency beacons are built with GPS receivers which can locate position within a few meters. Search and rescue satellites are launched in near polar orbits at an altitude of 1,000 km.

The Doppler Effect

The Doppler effect occurs when there is a shift in the frequency of a wave.

For example, suppose an ambulance is coming towards you with its siren blaring.

While you stand still, the ambulance moves towards you and then races away. At such times you must have noticed a change in the pitch of the siren. This change in pitch is caused by the Doppler effect.

The frequency of a sound wave determines the pitch. When the distance between the source of sound and the sound's observer varies, there is a shift in the frequency of the signal. This is known as the Doppler effect.

The search and rescue satellite (SARSAT) system is specially designed to help survivors during emergencies such as an air crash, shipwrecks and other accidents in remote areas. Speedy search and rescue operations are possible only when the exact location of the accident is known. Therefore, search and rescue satellites combine both aspects of both communication and position determination.

In case of an emergency, a user (ship or aircraft) continuously transmits a distress radio signal in a particular band, using a device known as the distress beacon. Along with the radio signal, the location of the accident and the identification number of the user are also transmitted. When a SARSAT satellite receives this signal, the location of the source of the signal or the location of the accident is determined to the accuracy of a few meters.

The information regarding the accident and its location is then passed on to the agency responsible for search and rescue operations. Since the time the SARSAT system became operational, hundreds of lives have been saved.

Saving Lives

ISRO's satellites also receive these distress signals. In August 1998, a twelve-member team of young mountaineers from the United Kingdom was on an expedition to the Himalayas. When the team was at a height of 16,000 feet north of Manali, a 16-year old girl suddenly fell sick because of a high-altitude breathing problem. The captain of the team activated their beacon transmitter to send a distress signal. An ISRO satellite received the signal and sent it to the SARSAT satellite system. The location of the team was then determined, and the Indian Air Force immediately rushed their rescue helicopter to the site. The sick girl was brought back to Manali and given emergency medical treatment. This timely help saved the life of the girl.

Scientific Satellites

India's first satellite, Aryabhata, was a scientific satellite. It was built to conduct experiments in X-ray astronomy, aeronomics, and solar physics. It had two telescopes, one for observing particular objects and the other on its belly for general scanning of the sky. Even during the short period of five days when the experiment was working, Aryabhata's detectors found evidence of X-rays at the centre of our galaxy.

Astronomy Satellites

An astronomy satellite is a big telescope floating in space. Astronomy satellites are in orbit just above Earth. They are put at this location so that the gases that make up Earth's atmosphere do not cloud the vision of the satellites, and the heat of Earth does not confuse the imaging equipment of the satellites. The satellite can also look up into space ten times better than a telescope of similar length located on Earth.

Astronomy satellites analyse the electromagnetic spectrum. By looking at different wavelengths of light—such as ultraviolet, x-ray, visible spectrum, microwaves and gamma rays—they generate pictures of things that are far away in space. These pictures are not like photographs from a regular camera, but images created from an analysis of electromagnetic waves. Astronomy satellites have many different applications. They can be used for making star maps. They can also be used to take pictures of planets in the solar system. They can be used to study mysterious phenomena such as black holes and quasars.

Black Holes

The life of a star can range from millions to billions of years. A black hole is formed by the collapse of a big star to such a dense state that nothing can free itself from its grip. Light cannot escape from a black hole. So a black hole is invisible, but its strong gravitational force is responsible for emitting X-rays.

Quasars

A quasar is a big energy source that gives out powerful X-rays and ultraviolet radiation. Quasars are believed to be the most distant objects known to man. One estimate is that they are eight thousand million light years away. In other words, the light from quasars takes billions of years to reach Earth.

DID YOU KNOW?

The Hubble Space Telescope is the most famous astronomy satellite in the world. It was launched by the United States in April 1990. It is a 12-tonne space telescope, orbiting at a height of 600 km. It is named after Edwin Powell Hubble, a famous astronomer. It is the largest astronomical telescope ever placed outside the atmosphere. It can capture stars that can be observed only faintly by ground-based telescopes. It provides a clear digital image with a resolution 7 to 10 times higher than that from a ground-based telescope. It has been designed in such a way that visiting astronauts can service it and replace failed parts. It has already been serviced several times and is still operational.

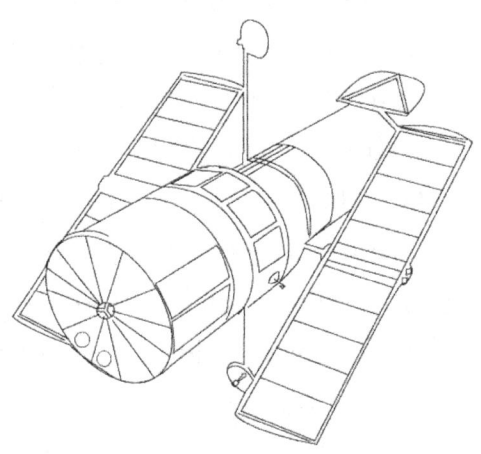

Hubble Space Telescope

India launched an astronomy satellite called ASTROSAT on September 20, 2015. This satellite works as a space-borne astronomy observatory.

Atmospheric Studies Satellites

Atmospheric studies satellites were some of the very first satellites to be launched into space. They are in the LEO so that they can study the Earth's atmosphere.

Alouette, a satellite launched by Canada, was the world's first atmospheric studies satellite. Scientists in Canada wanted to learn more about the aurora borealis (the northern lights) to find out how disturbances in the atmosphere not only create brilliant lights in the northern skies at night, but also disturb radio communications.

India launched Megha-Tropiques, an atmospheric studies satellite, on 14 October 2011. The satellite was built in collaboration with France. *Megha* in Sanskrit means cloud and *tropiques* in French means the tropics. It is a LEO satellite. Megha-Tropiques is used to study the systems that influence tropical weather and climate.

It provides scientific data on the contribution of the water cycle in the tropical atmosphere, information on water in clouds, water vapour in the atmosphere and rainfall.

Space Exploration Satellites

Space exploration satellites are not satellites in the strict sense of the term. Spacecraft is the general term that is used. This is because a satellite is defined as one that orbits something else. Space exploration satellites are actually space probes that travel deep into the solar system. On their journeys, they send back detailed pictures and other data of faraway planets and other celestial bodies. But these spacecrafts are very similar to orbiting satellites in their design and functions.

Space exploration spacecrafts can be of three kinds: a fly-by mission, an orbiter or a lander. A fly-by spacecraft travels on a path that is at a distance from the planet and while flying by, makes observations and takes photographs. An orbiting spacecraft goes in an orbit around the planet and the instruments in the spacecraft make observations and take photographs. A lander is first put in an orbit around the planet. Then a rover takes off and lands on the planet. The rover can travel over the surface of the planet and make observations. Curiosity is the latest rover launched by NASA to study Mars.

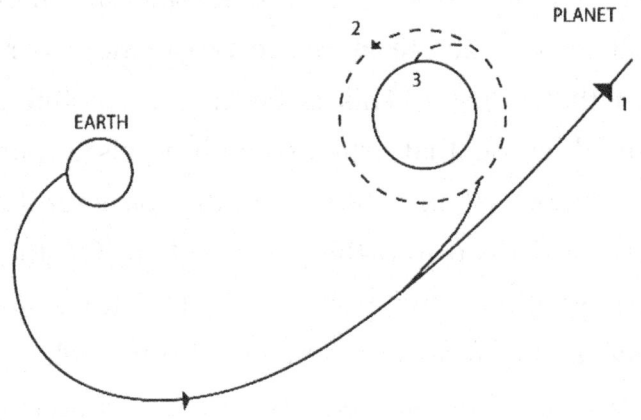

The Three Types of Spacecrafts:
1 – Fly-by Spacecraft, 2 – Orbiter, 3 – Lander

Numerous spacecrafts have been launched for exploration of the moon, the sun, other planets of the solar system, asteroids and comets. Chandrayaan-1, which was launched by ISRO in October 2008, was a space exploration satellite. The objective of the Chandrayaan-1 mission was to prepare a 3D atlas of the moon's surface, including a map showing how various minerals are distributed over the moon's surface and a map that shows the different geological areas clearly. The mission collected a lot of data that helped scientists prepare these maps, but more importantly, the mission found water, trapped a few millimetres under the lunar soil.

ISRO launched its spacecraft to Mars called Mars Orbiter Mission (MOM) on November 5, 2013. MOM carries five scientific instruments intended for various scientific studies. The methane sensor on MOM is aimed at detecting the existence of methane, on Mars, which will provide the evidence for the theory of the presence of life on Mars.

ISRO proposes to follow up the Chandrayaan-1 mission with Chandrayaan-2, which will have a lander and a rover. The idea is to develop a robotic rover that will take off from the orbiting spacecraft, land on the moon, and rove over the moon's surface. The rover will analyse the moon's surface and environment. The data that it collects will be transmitted to the orbiting spacecraft, which in turn will transmit it to the ground station.

5
What Are Satellites Made of?

Satellites are built for a broad variety of missions. Depending on the mission, a satellite has different elements. However, just as all automobiles have a chassis, an engine, fuel tanks and steering systems, all satellites have some elements that are common. It is the payload that is different, depending on the mission.

What does a satellite contain?

If we think of a satellite as a human body, the skeleton of the human body can be compared to the structure of a satellite. It provides a bone

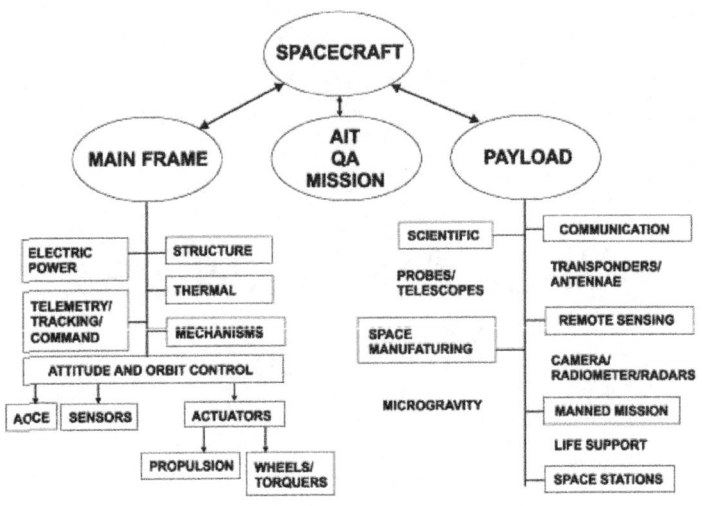

Spacecraft Elements

AIT stands for assembly, integration and testing. QA stands for quality analysis. The AIT QA mission is to put together all the elements to build the satellite while testing these elements to make sure that they are of good quality and reliable.

structure that takes all the load when we walk, run or jump. It houses all vital organs and protects them so that life is both regulated and preserved.

Similarly, a satellite has several systems and sub-systems that help regulate and preserve the life of the payload. The structure of the satellite provides a strong and stable platform to house the payload, systems and sub-systems of the satellite. It houses everything that is kept inside the satellite. It needs to be strong so that it can withstand the shocks and vibrations at the time of the launch of the satellite. It also provides protection from the harsh conditions in space — vacuum, extreme temperatures and radiation.

The weight of the structure should be low. That is why materials that have low weight but high strength are used. It is also important that they retain their strength and shape throughout the time that the satellite is in orbit. Aluminium honeycomb panels are most commonly used. Advanced composites like Carbon Fibre Reinforced Plastic (CFRP) are used to meet more stringent requirements.

Usually, the structure of the satellite looks like a six-sided box. Its faces are flat and are designated as North, South, East, West, Earth viewing and Anti-Earth viewing sides. The equipment is mounted on all sides. The primary structure is the central cylinder that is the main load-bearing element. The secondary structure consists of solar arrays, antennae, appendages and brackets. The secondary structure is connected to the primary structure by trusses and brackets.

It is necessary that the payload of the satellite is protected from objects travelling through space at great speed, such as small meteorites, space junk and charged particles. That is why the material used to cover the outside of the satellite has to be strong and resistant to puncture. Satellites often protect their payloads in small sturdy containers that cover the instruments.

Protection against Radiation

The sun emits high quantities of radiation. When we are in Earth's atmosphere, everything is protected from the harmful effects of the sun's radiation by the atmosphere. In space, where there is no atmosphere, satellites need to be protected from the sun's radiation. That is why satellites must use materials resistant to radiation so that the payload, which is sensitive to radiation, is adequately covered.

What powers the satellite?

The power systems in a satellite consist of:
- Solar Cells
- Battery
- Power Conditioning System

Solar Cells

The electrical and electronic systems in a satellite require power for their functioning. In a satellite, we get this power by converting sunlight into electric power. Nowadays, we have devices that tap solar energy for heating and lighting purposes in our houses. In a satellite, a similar device that can convert sunlight directly into electric power is used. This device is called the photovoltaic cell.

Satellites have high-efficiency photovoltaic solar cells for generating power. A single photovoltaic cell cannot produce much power. So, the solar panels of a satellite have hundreds of photovoltaic cells connected together. These solar panels generate enough electricity to provide power to the satellite's computers, radios, cameras and other equipment. They also recharge the back-up batteries of the satellite.

Battery

Orbiting satellites sometimes go behind Earth with respect to the sun. This is called eclipse, which can happen in every orbit or seasonally, depending on the type of orbit. Eclipse occurs when spacecrafts orbit around Mars, the moon and other planets as well.

During an eclipse, the solar panel is not in a position to function because it does not get light from the sun. So the satellite carries a battery to supply power when the solar panel does not get light. Nickel Hydrogen and Lithium-ion batteries are used in space. For long voyages, fuel cells and nuclear power sources are also used.

The demands of power during an eclipse depend on the orbit of the satellite. If the satellite is in the geosynchronous orbit (35,786 km), eclipse occurs twice a year, in spring and autumn. Each eclipse season lasts for 45 days, and the duration of the eclipse varies from day to day. On the first day of the season, the eclipse lasts only for three minutes. It gradually increases to a maximum of 72 minutes on the twenty-third day of the season that is known as the equinox day (21st March and 21st September). It again decreases to three minutes on the last day of the season.

The number of eclipses increases as the height of the orbit decreases. For the LEO (550 km), there are about 15 eclipses per day or about 5,500 orbits a year. The batteries are discharged during the eclipse period and are recharged when there is sunlight.

How does the satellite stay in correct position?

For certain functions, the satellite needs to be oriented in a specific direction. This process is called stabilization.

Stabilization

A satellite needs to be stable and pointing in the desired direction so that it can take precise measurements from its place in the orbit. Satellites are stabilized so that they do not wobble.

What happens if a satellite is not stabilized? The satellite's measurements and pictures will be inaccurate and fuzzy. The orbit of the satellite will slowly change course either towards Earth or out into space.

There are two ways to stabilize a satellite:

(a) Spin Stabilization and (b) Three-axis Stabilization.

Spin Stabilization

A simple way of stabilizing a satellite is to spin the satellite along its axis. The entire satellite spins except for the antenna and the camera, which are mounted on a de-spinning platform, so that they can see the desired object continuously. Spinning can be achieved by using rods with coils of wire around them. A current passed through the rods creates magnetic fields round the wires. When the rod's magnetic field interacts with Earth's magnetic field, the rod begins to spin. If we have rods in three opposing directions, we can have the satellite spin in all three axes: up, down and out.

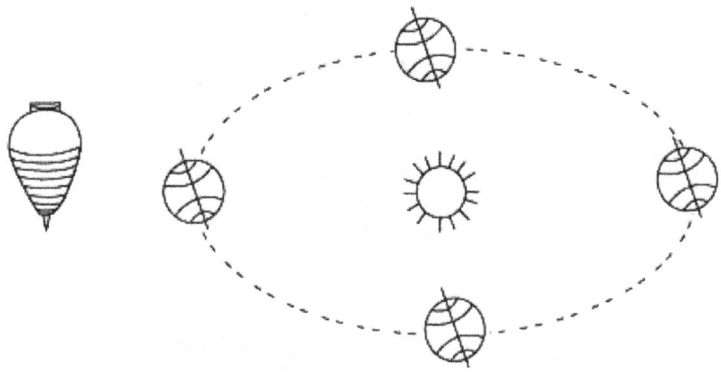

Examples of stabilization by spinning:
(a) A spinning top keeps its axis vertical.
(b) The spinning Earth always keeps its north axis pointing towards the pole star.

Stabilization by Spinning

The advantage of a spin-stabilized satellite is that it requires very little power. But the disadvantage is that the satellite cannot collect full power all the time because only one third of the solar cells see sun in every rotation.

Three-axis Stabilization

Three-axis stabilization is when the satellite as a whole points stably in one direction. This is achieved by rotating reaction/momentum wheels at much higher speed than the rotation of a spin satellite. The wheels hold the momentum along each axis providing stabilization to the satellite

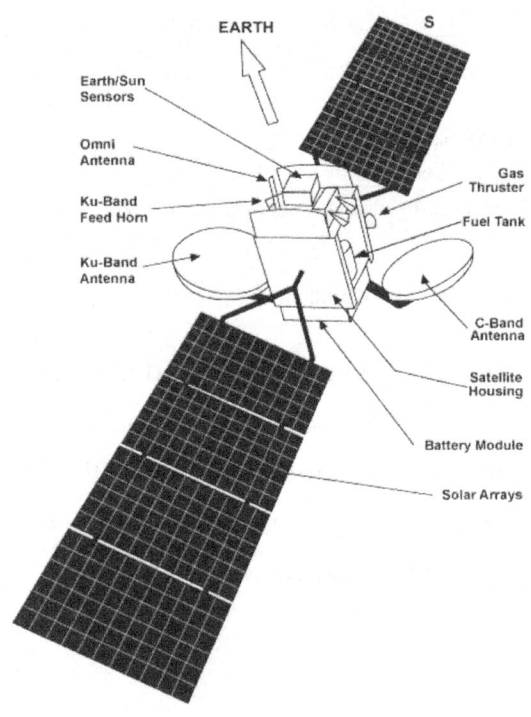

Three-axis Stabilized Satellite

as a whole. Here, large solar panels are used for generating enough power required for the satellite. These panels track the sun continuously and generate full power. The solar panels are kept folded during launch and deployed once the satellite separates from the rocket.

Gyroscopes, which work on the principle of a spinning top, provide the angle, body rate and orientation information in space. Small rockets called thrusters, which are mounted on the satellite, are used to correct the spin rate, spin axis and spin direction.

Where is the satellite looking?

The position of a satellite in space and the direction it is facing is called **attitude**. The attitude determines what a satellite looks at: which way its cameras are facing and the angle the satellite makes with the object it is orbiting.

To understand this, think of the movements you make when you are watching a moving object. We rotate our neck as much as possible, and tilt our bodies. If we want to go on watching the moving object, we move the position of our leg and adjust it according to requirement. Similarly, the satellite antenna has to look at a spot on Earth for maximum efficiency. The attitude and orbit control system (AOCS) makes sure that a satellite is in the desired orbital position and maintains its orientation towards Earth continuously.

On the whole, the idea is that a satellite should remain steady while it is orbiting. The stability of a satellite in space is subject to a variety of disturbances caused by solar radiation pressure, Earth's magnetic field, the non-spherical property of Earth and even movements within the satellite itself. Such control is achieved in several ways by the AOCS through sensors and processing computers.

Sensors

Sensors are an important part of the attitude control system. Earth sensors, sun sensors, and star sensors are the important sensors used in most satellites. They provide vital inputs to the AOCS for determining orientation.

Earth Sensors

The infrared detector on Earth sensors senses the difference in temperature between Earth and space, and this difference is processed to determine the attitude of the satellite. With the help of Earth Sensors, the satellite continuously locks on Earth and tracks it so that the Earth-viewing face of the satellite always sees Earth. Imagine how the security cameras lock onto moving objects and keep tracking them.

Sun Sensors

A Sun Sensor consists of a silicon solar cell. Whenever light falls on the cell, it converts the solar radiation into an electrical signal that can be of two types: analog and digital. An analog Sun Sensor is used for pointing one of the satellite axes towards the sun so that the solar panels can be continuously pointed in the direction of the sun. The digital Sun Sensor is used to measure the sun's angle with reference to the satellite's axes.

Star Sensors

Stars provide very accurate references for finding direction. The Star Sensor detects the stars in its field of view and sends the information for comparison with the star catalogue stored in the computer. Once the stars are located, the output gives the direction of the satellite with respect to those stars.

The Sun Sensors and Star Sensors are useful for determining the direction of the satellite in space when it is injected from the rocket as well as during orbit correction manoeuvres.

Orbit Control

The orbit of a satellite often gets disturbed due to atmospheric drag, solar wind and radiation pressure, magnetic fields, impact of meteorites and the gravitational forces of nearby planets. Typically the orbit is corrected at 2-3 month intervals. Orbit control is the process by which a satellite stays in its desired orbit. This is done by firing thrusters which are fixed on the satellites. Orbit control activities are carried out by scientists/system experts by giving commands from the ground station.

Thrusters

Thrusters contain compressed gas which, when released, moves the satellite to correct its direction. The force of the compressed gas (the action) causes the satellite to move in the opposite direction (the reaction).

Orbit Raising

The low earth orbiting satellites are launched into their destined orbits by rockets. However, the satellites which are intended for higher orbits are launched into intermediate orbits by the rockets and subsequently transferred to their destined orbits by firing the engines on the satellite. Orbit transfer is important particularly for satellites that are placed in the GSO orbit. Geostationary satellites reach their orbit in two stages. First, the satellite is taken to an orbit with perigee at 200 km and apogee at 36,000 km. This is called the Geostationary Transfer Orbit (GTO). The satellite is then transferred to the GSO by firing the rocket engine that is fixed on the satellite. Such a rocket engine is called the Liquid Apogee Motor (LAM) since it uses liquid propellants.

How does the satellite communicate?

A satellite sends information about the functioning of its systems to the ground station through a process called telemetry. Using telemetry, the staff in the satellite control centre assesses the health of the satellite and its performance. The satellite control centre sends certain instructions to the satellite using the ground station. This is called telecommand. In addition, the ground station tracks the satellite by sending a particular radio signal (radio tones) and receiving it from the satellite. This tracking process, known as ranging, provides the data for determining the orbit of the satellite precisely. The orbit of a satellite is represented using a set of parameters against time. It is called ephemeris.

Telemetry

The telemetry system gathers information about the voltage and current condition of power subsystems, the temperature of critical subsystems, fuel tank pressures, the status of switches and relays in the communication system and the AOCS and transmits the information to the ground station in a particular format.

Telecommand

A command is an instruction to the satellite to change its settings or to perform certain functions. A command from the satellite control centre is sent to an Earth station and then transmitted to the satellite. The command receiver in the satellite receives the signal, decodes it and sends a verification signal to the ground. After verification, an execute signal is sent from the control centre. The satellite receives the signal, decodes it and distributes it to the appropriate subsystem in the satellite. Using telecommand, we can operate any instrument inside the satellite.

Tracking

Tracking consists of finding out the current orbit position and movement of the satellite. It determines the position of the satellite and this information is used to calculate future orbital motion. Multiple ground stations are used for determining the precise orbital position and trajectory of the satellite.

Antennae

All satellites need to have some means of communication with Earth. This is necessary because the satellite needs to receive instructions and transmit the information it collects. This is done by using an antenna. An antenna is a piece of equipment that allows transmission and reception of radio signals. Since information is transmitted by using radio waves, the antenna directs the energy of radio wave in a desired direction.

An antenna can be simple, like the radio antenna we see on the top of a car or those seen on older television sets. But they need to be very long to pick up signals. Long antennae can be a problem because the satellite itself has to be as small as possible to make its launching easy and cheap. Transmitting signals by using a simple antenna is also inefficient because the signal is emitted in a spherical fashion. Using a simple antenna would mean that half of the radio waves would be sent backwards into empty space.

That is why dish antennae are used on satellites. A parabolic dish reflects all radio waves that enter the dish into a single point. This single point is called the focus. A receiving horn (feed) is built around this focus. It gathers signals reflected to it so that an internal computer can process these signals. Similarly, the signals from the satellite are sent through the feed, which are reflected off the dish and sent down to Earth. The dish antenna works like a torch directing light in a particular direction.

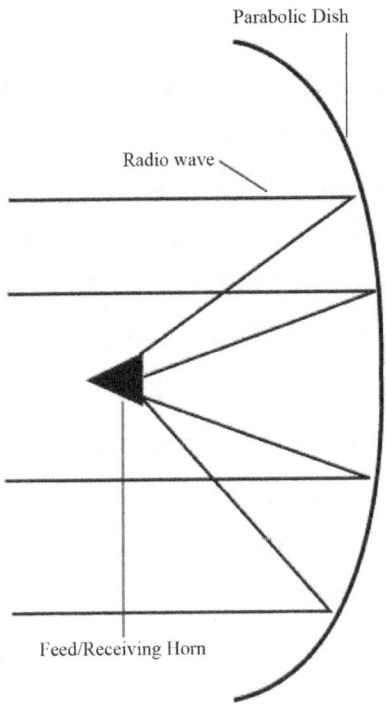

How Dish Antenna Works

Solid State Recorder

The solid state recorder is a memory device which stores digital data in a particular format. It uses semiconductors to record data and replay the data like in a mobile phone. It has the ability to simultaneously record data and play it back. Generally remote sensing satellites carry the recorder to store the data onboard and download it whenever there is visibility to ground station.

How does the satellite stay cool?

For any machine, even the human body, to function properly, it has to be at a correct temperature and stay at that temperature. This is called thermal control. The human body has a very sophisticated thermal control system. Heat is distributed in our bodies by circulation of blood which acts like heat pipes inside the body. It helps maintain the temperature of all our vital organs at a constant temperature, irrespective of the outside environment. We assist the thermal control system of our body by wearing woollen clothes in the cold or light-coloured cotton clothes during summer.

Like in the human body, the temperature of the various parts of a satellite has to be controlled. The thermal control system in a satellite maintains the temperature of its different subsystems. The thermal control methods used in a satellite include thermal systems with heat shield, multi-layer insulation blankets, heaters and thermal control coatings. Heat pipes filled with fluid are also used inside the satellite for thermal control.

For example, when satellites are in space, one side of their body faces the sun and the other side faces the chilling cold of space. The side of the satellite facing space would be several hundred degrees colder than the side facing the sun. Thermal blanketing is used to keep the satellite cooler or warmer, depending on what is needed. It acts like the insulation in a building: when it is hot outside, insulation keeps it cool and when it is cold outside, insulation keeps it warm inside.

Electrical charges can build up in satellite. When an electrical charge builds up in one area of the satellite, it can be dangerous to the equipment of the satellite. Electrical charges build up because material used in that area is highly conductive and since there is no air in space, there is no way for the electrical charge to move around. To get rid of the build-up of electrical charge, space scientists use conductors. These conductors are put on satellites in areas where charges are likely to build up. The wires of the conductors lead the charge away from that particular area of the satellite.

How does the satellite do its job?

The payload on a satellite is the equipment that performs the functions the satellite was sent up for. The type of payload that the satellite carries depends on its mission. For example, for a communication satellite, the payload has communication equipment (called transponders which receive signals from Earth, amplifies them and sends them back to earth) and antennae.

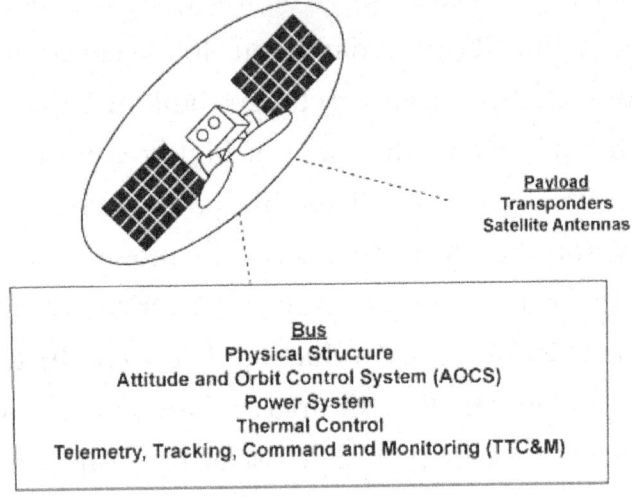

Communication Satellite Subsystems

DID YOU KNOW?

In a remote sensing satellite, the cameras are the payload.

In a meteorological satellite, the Very High Resolution Radiometer (VHRR) is the payload.

For a scientific satellite, the payload has scientific instruments like detectors and sensors that identify various minerals and signatures of radiations. For example, the Chandrayaan-1, a space exploration satellite, had the payload.

How is a satellite built?

All the elements we have described so far are put together and finally assembled into a satellite. When they are put together, they undergo extensive and rigorous testing. These tests are necessary because, once the satellite is put into space, it is not easy to make repairs to its parts. That is why we have to make sure that all the equipment in the satellite are reliable and of the best quality.

It is also necessary to test the equipment in an environment that the satellite will encounter in space. For this, space environment is artificially created in a laboratory and the equipment is tested under these conditions. One is the shock and vibration test, which is meant for conditions during the launch of a satellite, another is the temperature cycling test where the performance of the satellite is checked from high to low temperatures. If the equipment goes through these tests successfully, it is considered space-worthy.

The assembled satellite is then tested to demonstrate that the structure is good enough to handle the launch.

The assembly, integration and testing activities are conducted in a clean room which is an environmentally clean area designed to highest standards. In the clean room, it is required that dust particle of size 5 microns should be less than 100,000 in one cubic meter volume. This is achieved by using various filters for air conditioning. Air showers are used for cleaning people entering the clean room and for cleaning all the equipment entering the room. The height of the clean room is 10 m high and it is equipped with a crane that can lift things weighing up to 5,000 kg.

6
3, 2, 1...Take off!

How are satellites launched?

Isaac Newton had suggested that if a body were thrown from the top of a high mountain with sufficient speed in a direction parallel to Earth's surface, it would go around Earth. In other words, it would become a satellite of Earth.

Let us imagine that we climb an imaginary mountain whose summit stands out above Earth's atmosphere. The imaginary mountain would have to be about ten times higher than Mount Everest. If we throw a ball from this mountain top, it would fall to the ground in a curving path.

The faster we throw the ball, the farther it will go before it hits the ground. If we throw the ball at a speed of 27,359 km per hour, the ball would not reach the ground. It would circle Earth in a curved path and it would be in orbit. It would become a satellite of Earth.

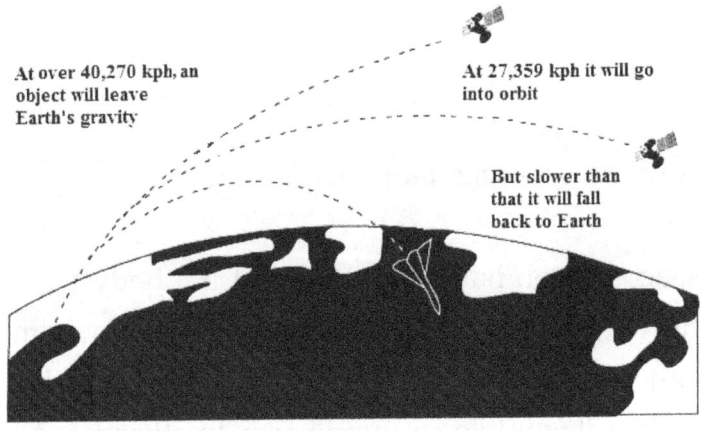

How Satellites Are Launched

The trick when launching a satellite is to get it high enough to do its job, but without losing the satellite to outer space. It is a delicate balance of push and pull caused by the inertia of the moving object and Earth's gravity. If we launch a satellite at 27,359 km per hour, the forward momentum will balance gravity and it will circle Earth. On the other hand, if the satellite is launched faster than 40,270 km per hour, it will leave the gravitational pull of Earth.

We need rockets to launch satellites because only rockets can propel the satellites at the required speed. Most rockets are chemical rockets that burn fuel. Fuel is combined with oxygen to produce energy and gases. Some of the energy is released as fire. Much of the energy is released as heat, and the heat causes the gases inside the rocket to expand rapidly. A small opening at the bottom of the rocket allows the heated gases to escape and in doing so, provide a thrust that propels the rocket in the opposite direction.

Balloons

To understand how a rocket works, think about what happens inside a balloon. Air is compressed by the balloon's rubber walls. The air pushes back so that the inward and outward pressing forces are balanced.

When the nozzle is released, air escapes through it and the balloon is propelled in the other direction. In rockets, the gas is produced by burning fuel.

In a rocket, one kind of energy is converted into another kind. In a chemical rocket, the chemical energy of the fuel is converted into kinetic energy. Most rockets use either solid fuel, liquid fuel or both. In a solid fuel rocket, the fuel and oxidizer are mixed into a solid form. In a liquid fuel rocket, the fuel and the oxidizer are in a liquid form and kept separately. The combination of the fuel and the oxidizer is called propellant.

The combustion chamber, the nozzle and the nose cone are important parts of a rocket. The propellant burns in the combustion chamber producing hot gas at high temperature. The nozzle expands the gas and produces thrust. The top portion of the rocket is called the nose cone. The satellite is kept in the nose cone. When the rocket goes up, the outer surface of the nose cone gets heated up because of friction with the atmosphere. To protect the satellite, the outer surface of the nose cone is made of special materials and is called the heat shield.

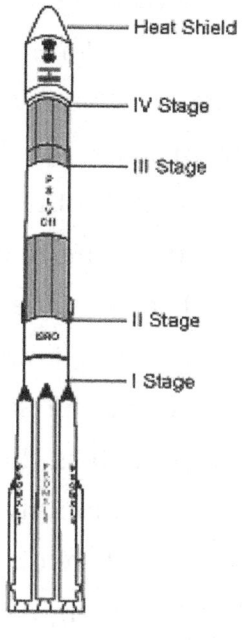

A Rocket

A rocket lifts off from the launch pad only when it expels gas out of its engine. The rocket accelerates upwards and travels away from Earth at a speed of 112 km per second or 40,270 km per hour. This allows the rocket to escape Earth's gravity.

The rocket slows down, but Earth's gravity never slows it down enough to cause it to fall back to Earth.

Large rockets, which carry satellites into deep space, have a problem. If they have to reach their destination, they will need a great deal of propellant. In that case, the tanks storing propellants, engines and other hardware will become larger, too. It is true that bigger rockets can travel greater distances than small rockets. But, if the rocket is too large, its structures become heavy, and in that case, the satellite it carries have to become smaller. It is difficult for rocket scientists to reduce the quantity of propellants. This means that the structure of the rocket needs to use stronger but lightweight material.

Another way to launch rockets is with stages. Each stage performs as a small rocket. When the stage is spent, the casing of the spent stage falls away and the next stage is fired. This method helps the rocket to go to higher altitudes while spending the fuel optimally.

In the sixteenth century, rockets were used as fireworks. Johan Schmidlap, a German fireworks manufacturer, invented the step-rocket. It was a multi-staged vehicle for lifting fireworks to higher altitudes. What it meant was that a large sky rocket (the first stage) carried a smaller sky-rocket (the second stage). When the large rocket burned out, the smaller rocket continued to climb to a higher altitude before showering the sky with glowing cinders.

Schmidlap's idea was adapted in modern rocketry to create all rockets that go into outer space today.

This technique of building a rocket is called staging. Begin with a big rocket, put a smaller one on top of it, put a still smaller rocket on top of the second one, put another rocket on the third one and then, the satellite on top of the fourth rocket. The diagram below shows how staging is done for the Polar Satellite Launch Vehicle (PSLV), one of India's successful rockets.

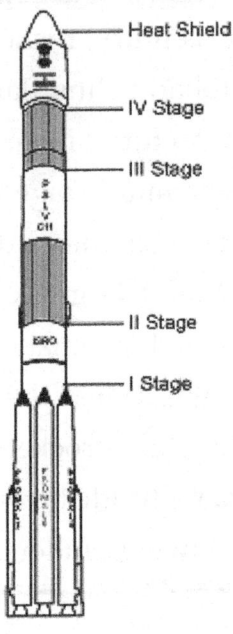

PSLV: Staged Rocket

In case of staging, the large rocket lifts its own weight and the weight of the other three. When the large rocket (first stage) is empty, it falls away. The second rocket (second stage) fires and accelerates itself to lift the third and fourth stages with the payload to higher altitudes. When it is empty, the third stage takes over. When the third stage spends itself, the fourth stage does its job by carrying the satellite to the necessary height. By staging, the mass of the rocket is reduced in flight, making the upper stages more efficient in doing their job. Also, thanks to staging, it becomes possible not only to reach the orbits around Earth but the moon and other planets, too.

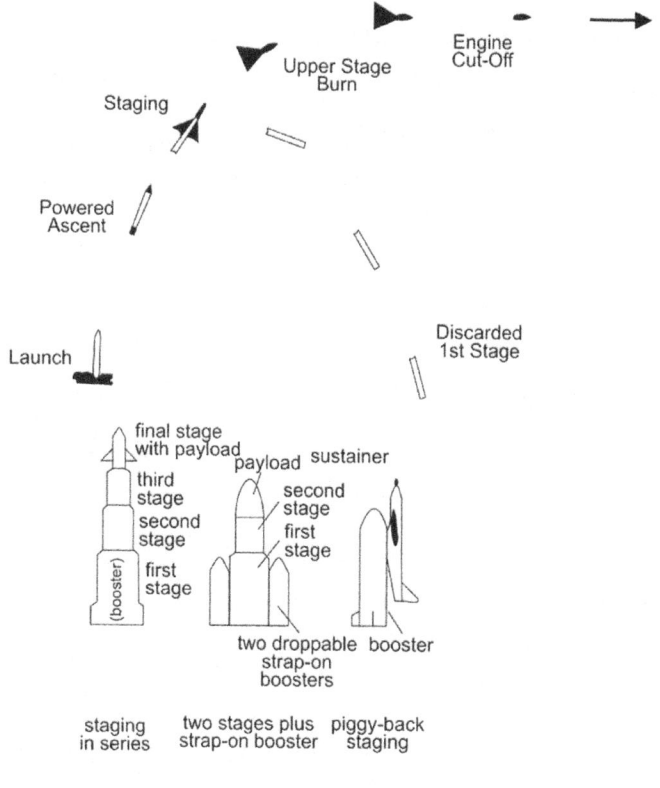

Flight to Orbit

When a satellite is launched by a multi-stage rocket, the rocket is fired in the vertical direction to start with. After the rocket passes through the dense layer of the lower atmosphere (about 120 km), a command from the ground is sent to the rocket and the heat shield is separated. The direction of the rocket is then turned towards east, so that it is parallel to Earth. The velocity of the rocket is such that it stays at the desired orbit at that height. The satellite then separates from the rocket and enters its orbit with the appropriate velocity. If the satellite is launched in the eastern direction, it gets the advantage of Earth's daily rotational speed from west to east.

If a satellite is to be placed in the polar orbit, it is necessary to launch the satellite towards north or south. But in that case, it is not possible to get the advantage of Earth's daily rotational speed. For example, the PSLV rocket is fired from Sriharikota (ISRO's launching station) to launch the satellite in the polar orbit. This is necessary because there is thickly populated land area in the northern direction, but in the southern direction, except for Sri Lanka, there is the vast stretch of the Indian Ocean.

The total time taken from the beginning of the launch till the satellite is put in its orbit is only a matter of a few minutes. After the satellite is put in its orbit with the appropriate velocity, it does not require additional propellant for its motion. It is a free ride. It is the initial velocity and the gravitational force of Earth that keep the satellite moving in the orbit. As long as the velocity of the satellite does not change, it continues to move in the orbit for a long time.

Since the launching of the satellite towards east is always helpful, it is necessary that the launching station is located at a place where there is a vast expanse of water in the east. India's satellite launching centre at Sriharikota on the Andhra coast is thus an ideal launching site.

What are India's satellite launch vehicles?

India has, at present, two operational launch vehicles: the Polar Satellite Launch Vehicle (PSLV) and the Geosynchronous Satellite Launch Vehicle (GSLV). Generally, PSLV carries satellites to the polar orbit while GSLV carries satellites to the geosynchronous orbit.

PSLV

PSLV was ISRO's first attempt to design and develop an operational launch vehicle that could be used to fly satellites to their orbit. PSLV is 44 m high and has a diameter of 2.8 m. It has a lift-off mass of 295 tonne. It has four stages, which use solid and liquid propulsion alternately. PSLV is unique in combining alternate solid and liquid stages.

PSLV was originally designed to launch satellites weighing about 900 kg into an orbit of 900 km. The first successful flight of PSLV was in October 1994 when it carried a satellite of 850 kg into orbit. Since that time, the weight that PSLV can carry has gradually increased from 850 kg to 1,600 kg.

The systems in PSLV are designed in such a way that it can serve more than one payload mission. The PSLV can now carry several satellites in a single flight and launch them to different orbits. In January 2007, PSLV carried four satellites including two foreign satellites. In April 2008, PSLV created a world record by carrying ten satellites in a single flight!

PSLV is a versatile vehicle, too. It can carry out missions to the polar orbit, the GTO or other orbits. It has already carried a large number of missions to the polar orbit. It also launched India's prestigious space missions—Chandrayaan-1 in October 2008 and the Mars Orbiter in November 2013.

GSLV

In PSLV, ISRO has created a versatile and reliable launch vehicle. But, even with PSLV, there was something missing in ISRO's range of rockets. ISRO had no muscle to climb to 36,000 km to carry its communication satellites. GSLV did that in 2001, making India the sixth country in the world to have that capability.

GSLV is 49 m high. It has a diameter of 2.8 m. It has a lift-off mass of 414 tonne. It is a three-stage launch vehicle. The first stage uses solid propellants. The second stage uses liquid propellants. The third stage uses cryogenic propellants.

GSLV-III is a launch vehicle currently under development at ISRO. It can launch heavy satellites into the GTO. It can put a satellite weighing upto 4,400 kg in the GSO.

What is orbit transfer?

In case of certain satellites, it becomes necessary to transfer them from one orbit to another. For example, a communication satellite is put in the GSO in two steps. In the first step, the satellite is launched in an elliptical orbit with perigee at about 200 km and apogee at about 36,000 km. This orbit is called the geostationary transfer orbit (GTO). The satellite is then transferred to the GSO by using a rocket motor fixed on the satellite. The rocket motor is called the Liquid Apogee Motor (LAM) because it uses liquid propellants. The liquid propellant for the LAM is stored in the satellite itself.

When the communication satellite is at the apogee, the LAM is fired through commands sent to the satellite from the ground station. The firing of the LAM is repeated until the satellite is closer to the GSO. Thus, the satellite is transferred from the GTO to an orbit called the drift orbit. Finally, the velocity is finely adjusted to make the satellite look stationary from Earth.

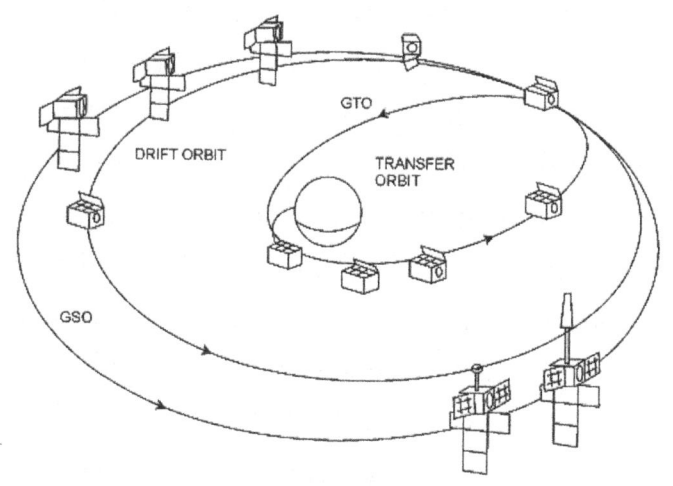

Orbit Transfer

Orbital transfers are also required when undertaking interplanetary missions. For example, when India took up its first mission to the moon (Chandrayaan-1), this became necessary. Chandrayaan-1 began its journey from Earth on a PSLV flight and first reached a highly elliptical initial orbit. In the initial orbit, the perigee was about 255 km and apogee was about 22,860 km. After orbiting Earth in its initial orbit for a while, Chandrayaan-1 spacecraft was taken to five more elliptical orbits whose orbits were progressively higher. This was done by firing the spacecraft's Liquid Fuel Engine (LFE) at opportune moments when the spacecraft was near the perigee.

As the spacecraft approached the apogee of its Earth orbit at 3,80,000 km, it passed at a distance of about 500 km from the moon since the moon had arrived there in its journey around Earth. At that time, the spacecraft's LFE was again fired. This slowed down the spacecraft sufficiently so that the gravity of the Moon could capture the spacecraft into an elliptical orbit.

After this, the height of the spacecraft's orbit was reduced in four steps. The Chandrayaan-1 spacecraft finally reached its intended lunar orbit of about 100 km from the moon's surface.

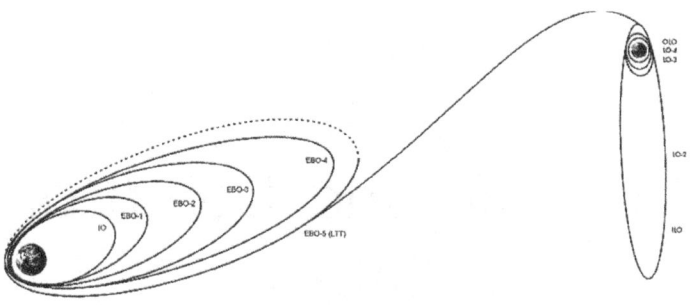

Orbit Transfer of Chandrayaan-1

On the whole, the launching of a satellite into orbit is a very complex and costly operation. Typically, the rocket that launches a satellite costs as much as the satellite itself. Every known engineering discipline is involved in building and flying a rocket, and that is why it is the common perception that rocket science is the most difficult science of them all.

7
The Life and Death of a Satellite

A satellite begins its life inside the fairing of a rocket that protects it from friction when the rocket climbs through Earth's atmosphere. It is mounted on a small fitting attached to the rocket, and it separates from the rocket by mean of a spring-loaded mechanism when it reaches its intended transfer orbit.

In the first few hours after the satellite separates from the rocket, it deploys its solar panels, adjusts its attitude with reference to Earth and the sun, and performs manoeuvres to reach its final orbit. These operations are a part of what is called the initial operation phase, which varies according to the mission of the satellite. In case of a satellite going to the LEO, it is put in an orbital trajectory close to the intended orbit, while in the case of a satellite meant for the GSO, it is put into a transfer orbit and subsequently, guided into the GSO.

When the satellite reaches the desired orbit, the in-orbit checkout phase starts, in which tests are carried out to reconfirm that the satellite is functioning with the expected performance based on ground tests. During the in-orbit checkout phase, the instruments of the satellite are switched on and tested. After completing in-orbit checkout, which generally lasts for a few weeks, the satellite is declared fit for service and begins performing its routine operations.

While in orbit, the satellite travels at a speed of 11,000 km to 28,000 km per hour, depending on its altitude. There are several things that disturb the satellite's orbit, and as a result, the satellite may undergo some deviation from its expected trajectory. Therefore, station-keeping operations are performed by space scientists to make necessary corrections to the orbit and attitude of the satellite throughout its mission so that it can continue to operate according to plan.

How long do satellites stay up in orbit?

Satellites stay in orbit for different periods of time depending on their orbits and their size and shape. In general, higher the orbit, the longer the satellites stay in orbit. At higher altitudes, where the vacuum of space is complete, there is almost no drag and that is why a satellite can stay in orbit for a long time. Satellites in the circular GSO — where they orbit along the equator — are likely to remain in space for a long time, and will stay in operation as long as their components continue to function.

At lower orbits, a satellite runs into traces of Earth's atmosphere that cause drag. Air molecules slow the satellite down and reduce the height of the orbit. When the orbit decays to a lower altitude where the atmosphere is denser, the satellite experiences more drag. Because the satellite is travelling at high speed, the friction with the air is enough to heat up the satellite and it eventually burns up and disintegrates. Large satellites which do not disintegrate this way are brought down through commands, and guided to fall in unpopulated areas such as oceans.

What is space debris?

Since the time the world's first satellite, the Sputnik-1, was launched in 1957, near space has become overcrowded with a large amount of debris. Satellite batteries that have exploded and parts of rockets still orbiting Earth form a huge garbage dump in space. These objects, both small and large, pose a danger to satellites because of the damage they might cause on collision.

When a satellite is launched in Earth orbit, the last stage of the rocket also keeps moving in the same orbit. If the orbit is at a height of 200 km to 300 km, the last stage of the rocket re-enters the atmosphere within a few days and burns out completely due to friction in the atmosphere. If the height of the orbit is about 900 km to 1000 km, the last stage of the rocket stays in the orbit for hundreds or thousands of years, because there is perfect vacuum at that height and therefore, no friction. Space debris also consists of old defunct satellites. Around the GSO, there are many old communication and weather satellites, which are not operational any more but are still in orbit, adding to the space debris at that height.

On occasion, satellites break apart due to explosion of propellant systems or engines. At least 160 satellites have broken up into smaller fragments. Sometimes, spy satellites are deliberately destroyed in space after their mission has failed so that it remains a secret. The fragmented pieces of these spy satellites have added to the space debris considerably. In 1985, during the test phase of the American Star Wars programme, a satellite was smashed by an anti-satellite weapon, creating 285 pieces of space debris.

Debris in space comes from many sources. Rockets used only once can remain in orbit, as can pieces of satellites or apparatus ejected intentionally so that they do not enter the wrong orbit. Things that fall out of an astronaut's hand can also become space debris! In 1965, astronaut Edward White lost a glove while performing a space walk in the vicinity of the Gemini capsule. The glove kept orbiting Earth for a month at a speed of 28,000 km per hour.

Suppose an astronaut doing repair in space drops a wrench. The wrench then goes into orbit, probably at a speed of something like 30,000 km to 70,000 km per hour. If the wrench hits any spacecraft carrying a human crew, the result would be disastrous. Space debris also consists of miscellaneous objects like nuts, bolts and spanners, inadvertently lost in space by astronauts during their space walk. There are also flakes of paint peeled off from the outer surface of satellites and a large number of particles of aluminium oxide produced from the combustion of solid propellant rockets.

Any small object that makes up space debris, travelling at a speed of about 8 km to 10 km per second, is dangerous. Collision with such an object may incapacitate even destroy an operational satellite. There is evidence of one working satellite becoming useless due to collision with space debris. In 1996, a small French satellite was totally damaged due to collision with the last stage of an Ariane rocket that had been discarded in space earlier. For an astronaut on a space walk, such collision may puncture a hole in his space suit and he may die due to lack of oxygen. Remember the movie *Gravity* and the havoc caused by space debris in it?

Space Walk

When an astronaut goes out from the spacecraft into open space it is called space walk. The astronaut must wear a spacesuit during the space walk so that he can survive in the hazardous conditions of space. A spacesuit is made of several layers of special fabric. The inner layers of the space suit consist of many layers of thin tubes, through which warm or cold water is continuously circulated to keep body temperature constant.

The outer layer of the spacesuit is designed to protect the astronaut from the fierce heat of the sun. The astronaut gets air for breathing through cylinders strapped to his back. The astronaut uses his own life support system and a set of tiny thrusters which can propel the unit in any direction. The astronauts uses the system for various types of tasks, such as repairing malfunctioning satellites, installing new equipment on satellites and building space stations like the International Space Station. In fact, the use of the term 'space walk' is confusing because an astronaut cannot really walk in space because of his weightless condition. He merely floats in space, and his speed is the same as that of the spacecraft.

Space debris has been the reason for quite a few space casualties. In 1983, the Space Shuttle

Challenger was hit by a piece of space debris which made a dent in its windshield. Afterwards, the cosmonauts on the Soviet space station Salyut 7 reported that one of its windows was hit by space debris. In 1988, the Mir space station was hit by an object, damaging one of the windows. Space debris is the reason why space shuttles orbit with their windows to the rear. This protects the astronauts on board, at least to some degree.

There are more than 30,000,000 objects in space which are less than 1 cm. These small particles can cause only superficial damage. There are more than 2,00,000 objects which are from 1 cm to 10 cm. These particles can cause holes in a satellite on collision. There are about 16,000 objects that are more than 10 cm. These objects can cause irreparable damage and are catalogued and tracked from Earth.

Since the beginning of the space age in 1957, more than 25,000 objects have been

Space Debris

launched in the near Earth orbit. With increasing space activity, the near Earth environment is facing the problem of space debris, which is getting more serious with time. There is an increase of about 2 to 5 per cent in space debris every year. It is estimated that by the year 2018, there would be about 96,000 large objects in the form of space debris in the near Earth space within 500 km altitude. Obviously, this will create a huge traffic jam in space.

What can be done to reduce the space debris in space?

There is no easy way to clear the debris from space. It has been proposed that deliberate explosion of on-orbit satellites should be stopped. After a satellite is launched in its orbit, the unspent propellant in the last stage should be drained off in space so that accidental explosion is avoided. It has also been proposed that, after a satellite in near Earth orbit stops functioning, it should be brought down to lower orbit in a controlled manner, so that it re-enters the atmosphere, and is destroyed. The non-functional satellites in the GSO should be shifted to a much higher orbit, so that the GSO is not cluttered with defunct satellites.

It has also been suggested that to reduce the impact of collision with space debris, the outer surface of satellites should be sufficiently strengthened. In any case, as a precautionary measure, most satellites are now heavily insured against possible damage by space debris.

How is space debris tracked?

There are many organizations that track space debris. For example, the US Space Surveillance Network (SSN) has established 31 ground-based radars and 16 large optical telescopes at different locations around the globe to monitor objects in space between altitudes of 200 km and 2000 km. With the help of this network, it is possible to monitor objects larger than 10 cm. According to this network, the number of such objects orbiting

Earth are more than 11,000. Of these, only 5 per cent are operational satellites.

The European Space Agency tracks more than 7,500 objects larger than 10 cm. An organization called North American Air Defense (NORAD) tracks all satellites bigger than a football. Amateurs have also been tracking satellites for several decades now. The Radio Amateur Satellite Corporation (AMSAT), which is an organization of ham radio operators worldwide, tracks specific satellites of interest.

8
The Story of India's Satellite Missions

Which was India's first satellite?

India's space programme started soon after Independence. Despite not having any existing infrastructure, Indian space scientists and administrators thought up a far-sighted space and satellite programme that continues to flourish today.

The first satellite that India built was Aryabhata. It was named after India's great astronomer, Aryabhata, who was born in Kerala in 476 AD. He was the first Indian who understood Earth's movement around its axis.

Aryabhata weighed 356 kg, and was the heaviest for the first attempt by any country. It was launched into a circular orbit of 600 km. It took 96.36 minutes to complete an orbit. It was a scientific satellite designed to conduct experiments in solar physics. The designed life of the satellite was six months. It was designed and built by Indian scientists and engineers in Peenya, a suburb of Bangalore.

Aryabhata was launched from the Soviet Union on April 19, 1975. It was a red letter day in India's space history. A Soviet rocket carrying the satellite was launched at 2300 hrs, Indian Standard Time. An hour and 40 minutes later, the satellite was sighted over Bears Lake near Moscow by a control station set up and manned by Indian engineers. Ten minutes later, the ISRO launching station at Sriharikota confirmed the signals.

Building the Aryabhata satellite was a spectacular achievement. In 1972, when the work on Aryabhata was started, there was no laboratory, no infrastructure and no expertise to build a satellite. Teams had to be assembled; the satellite had to be designed, built, tested and launched. All this was done in thirty months' time.

Weight of Aryabhata

Why was the weight of Aryabhata fixed at 356 kg? The story goes that Vikram Sarabhai, who was the chairman of ISRO, had gone to see the Soviet ambassador. The Soviet ambassador told him that the Soviet Union would be happy to launch Aryabhata. Sarabhai asked the ambassador what the weight of the first satellite that China had built was. The ambassador said that it was 165 kg. So Sarabhai decided that the weight of Aryabhata, India's first satellite, would be more than double the weight of the first Chinese satellite.

With the launching of Aryabhata, India became the eleventh nation in the world and the third in Asia—after Japan and China—to send its own satellite into space. Aryabhata served as the blueprint for ISRO to build its future satellites. With the successful launch of Aryabhata, India entered the space age.

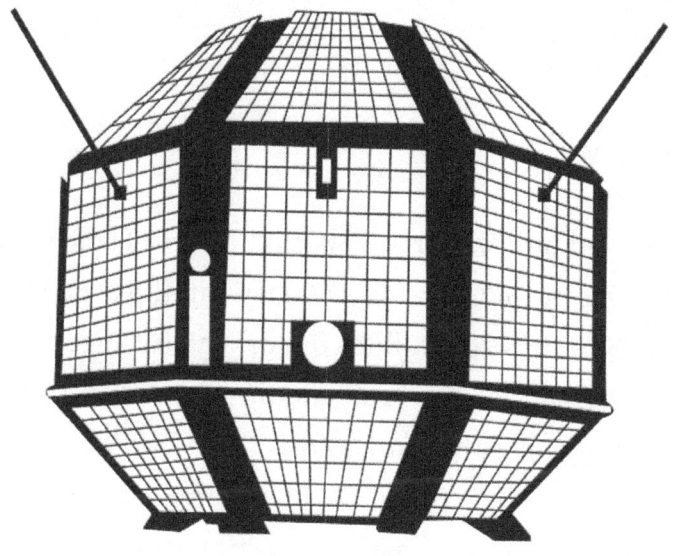

The Aryabhata Satellite

Today, the range and variety of ISRO's satellite technology is at par with international standards. ISRO is the world leader in remote sensing technology, with over 48 satellites successfully launched into orbit. ISRO has also built a large number of communication and weather satellites. It now has one of the biggest communication satellite systems in the world, its reach extending from Europe to Australia and Japan. ISRO has satellite capabilities that are comparable to the best anywhere in the world.

What is the INSAT system?

The Indian National Satellite (INSAT) System consists of ISRO's geostationary satellites. Started in 1983, it has 26 satellites out of which 11 satellites are in service now. These satellites provide services such as telecommunications, TV broadcasting, search and rescue, radio networking, weather forecasting and disaster warning operations.

Telecommunications

A total of about 1100 Earth stations and nearly 2,00,000 Very Small Aperture Terminals (VSATs) operate on the INSAT telecommunications network. The VSATs are very small terminals with antennae between the sizes of 1.2 to 2.5 m, located at the premises of the users. They provide voice, video, fax, data and multimedia services. The advent of VSATs in the 1980s gave a big boost to satellite-based data and business communication networks in India.

TV Broadcasting

The most dramatic impact of the INSAT system has been in the huge expansion of television coverage in India. Before the INSAT system was established, TV service was very limited. For example, in 1962, there were only 41 television sets in the country and only one TV channel. Today, there are 134 million households (out of 223 million households in the entire country) with television sets. Of this, over 103 million households have access to cable TV or satellite TV. This includes 40 million households that subscribe to DTH. India now has over 500 TV channels covering all the main languages spoken in the country. The number of TV channels is expected to grow to 1,000 in the coming years.

Search and Rescue

Ships, aircraft and people going on expedition carry emergency beacons. These beacons get activated in distress conditions and send signals with their identity and position to the satellites. The Search and Rescue transponders of INSAT satellites have picked up many distress signals and saved as many as 2,000 lives in the Indian region through timely search and rescue operations. Thus, satellite-aided search and rescue is an important tool for saving the lives of people affected by ship, aircraft and other disasters.

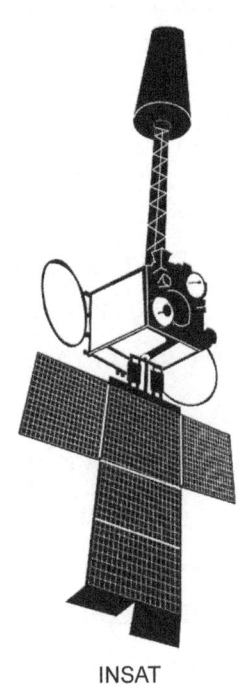
INSAT

Satellite News Gathering

This covers on-the-spot gathering of news by television channels. Satellites of the INSAT system help TV news agencies to gather news through small antennae on vans which can be driven anywhere and deployed in less than half an hour. This has now become a major service to broadcast news in real time.

Weather Services

INSAT satellites also provide data for weather forecasting. At present, there are more than a thousand data collection platforms aided by satellites. These are called Automatic Data Collection Platforms. The satellites also collect and send weather imagery. Three of the satellites of the INSAT system — INSAT-3A, INSAT-3D and Kalpana 1 — provide meteorological services by sending weather imagery and relaying weather data which is collected by Automatic Data Collection Platforms established in different parts of the country.

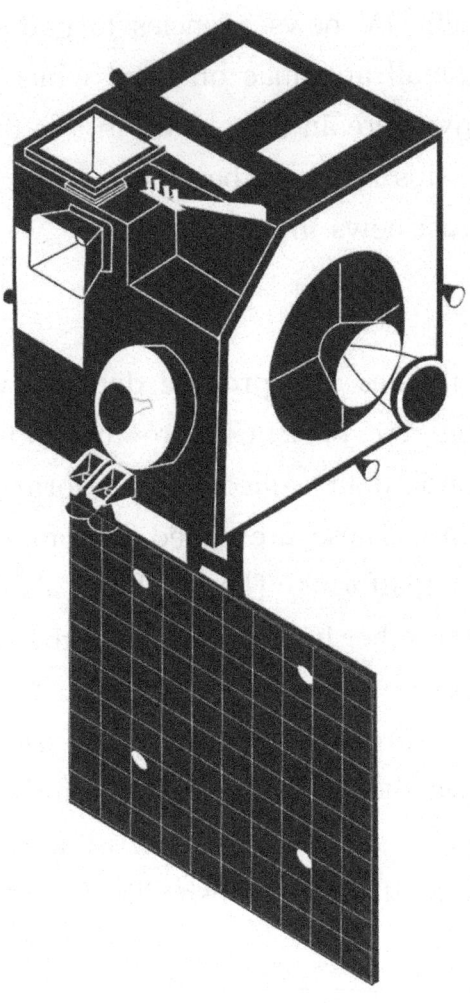

Kalpana 1

Disaster Warning Services

A highly innovative use of the INSAT system is the implementation of the disaster warning system that sends disaster-warning signals to areas affected by cyclone or floods. This is done through 350 receivers located in disaster-prone villages of the coastal region. Such warning helps the local authorities to start timely rescue or evacuation measures in these areas. The implementation of disaster warning services by ISRO has saved thousands of life and livestock.

Can statellites do more?

There are quite a few community services offered by the satellites of the INSAT system.

Tele-education

India launched a dedicated satellite called EDUSAT for promoting education. It is the first country in the world to have such a satellite. The objective of having a satellite dedicated to education is to share the scarce resources available in the country for teaching. For example, using EDUSAT, the best teachers in the country can teach students virtually in remote villages. The idea is to create interactive classrooms by bridging distance.

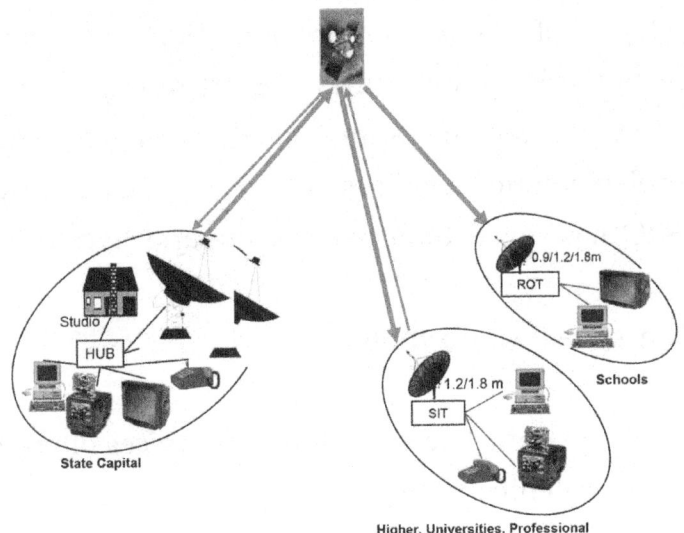

EDUSAT

Currently, about 55,000 classrooms from primary to the university level, as well as non-formal educational sector, are in the EDUSAT network, providing quality education to students in semi-urban and rural areas.

Telemedicine

India's communication satellites have also helped in providing quality healthcare services to rural India. At present, 306 health units located in remote rural areas and 16 mobile telemedicine units are connected to 60 speciality hospitals on the ISRO telemedicine network.

The idea of ISRO's telemedicine system is to provide healthcare from a distance. The telemedicine system has two ends. One is the specialist end, and the other, the patient's end. Through a satellite, the specialist doctor advises patients, non-specialist doctors, or even the paramedic at the patient's end about necessary medical care to be given to patients. The patient's information and clinical data are captured at the patient's end and transferred through satellite to the specialist's end. The specialist looks at the data and provides advice. ISRO's satellites have, thus, linked city speciality hospitals to health centres in rural areas and tiny towns, bringing to them the skills of specialists who work only in the big cities.

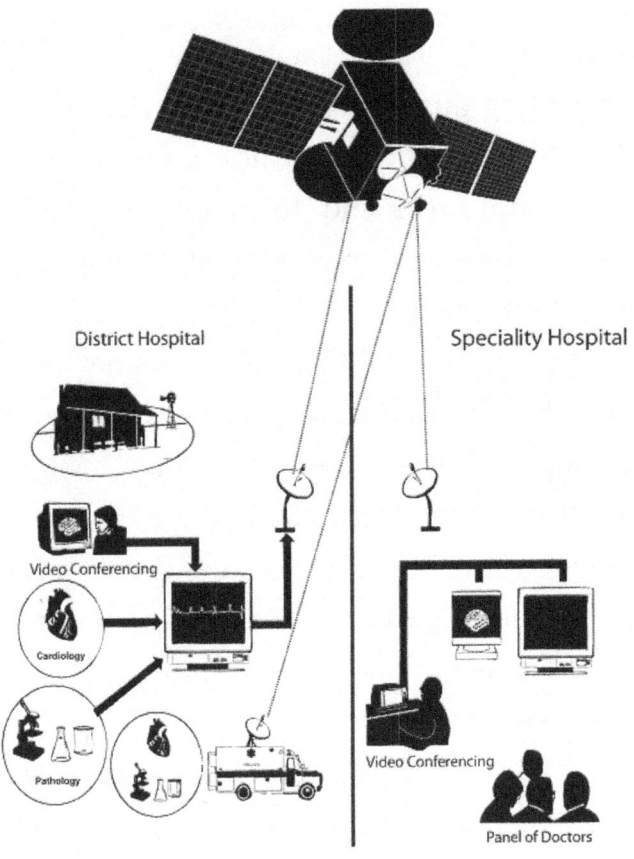

The Concept of Telemedicine

Development Communication

Using satellites, ISRO has made it possible for experts sitting in district or state headquarters to interact with villagers in remote rural areas on subjects that affect their lives. It started with the Satellite Instructional Television Experiment (SITE) programme in 1975. In that programme, ISRO put 2,400 TV sets in clusters of villages in six states of India. Through these TV sets, ISRO broadcast programmes to these villages through a satellite. These programmes were about agriculture, animal husbandry, dairy, poultry, health and hygiene, family planning and education. Some entertainment programmes were also included. These programmes were in the local language and broadcast for four hours every day.

The villagers were illiterate and from the poorer sections of the society. They had never read the newspapers or gone to the cinema. They had not even listened to a radio programme. The impact of the SITE programme was so good that

ISRO decided to expand such programmes in many parts of the country.

Village Resource Centre

Encouraged by the success of its development communication, tele-education and telemedicine programmes, ISRO started the Village Resource Centre (VRC) programme in 2004. In this programme, ISRO's satellites take the benefits of space technology directly to the doorsteps of rural India through the VRC located in the villages.

The VRC is a facility established for the common villager so that he can have access to specific information on the natural resources of his village in the local language and in local context for the overall development of the village. The VRC provides multiple services to the villagers such as tele-agriculture services, telemedicine, tele-education, telehealth, telefisheries and other such expert advice for the benefit of the local people. 473 VRCs have been set up throughout the country.

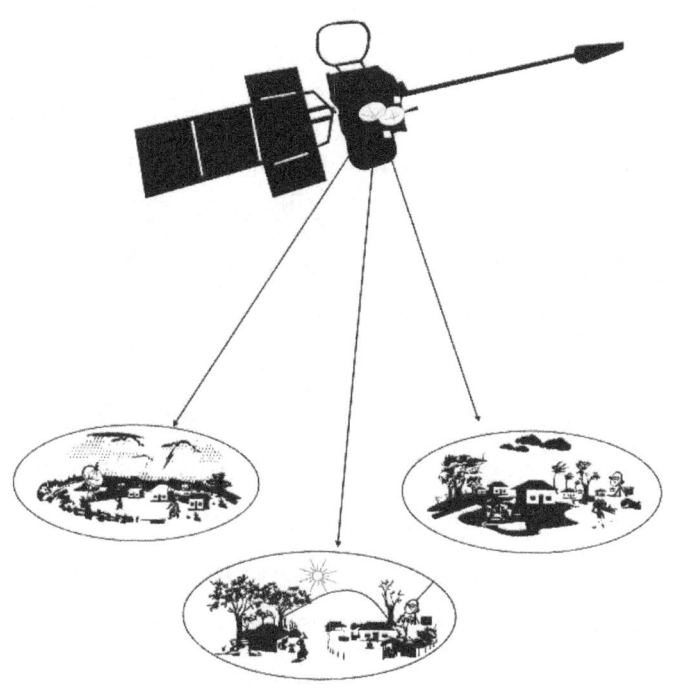

Village Resource Centre

Indian Remote Sensing Satellite System (IRS)

The Indian Remote Sensing Satellite System (IRS) was established in 1988. The IRS has nine remote sensing satellites and is the world's largest constellation in remote sensing. The satellites of the IRS are easily the most versatile civilian satellites for looking at Earth and its oceans. Imageries sent by these are used in various sectors of the country including agriculture, water resources, ocean resources, land use/land cover, forestry and disaster management. They are also marketed all over the world.

Using remote sensing data, ISRO assesses damage caused by floods, maps areas which run the risk of being flooded, identifies forest fires, and monitors underground coal fires. During floods, ISRO generates flood maps very quickly, identifying marooned areas for rescue and relief. ISRO has created a digital database depicting areas vulnerable to disasters such as cyclones, floods, drought, landslides and earthquakes. The database helps in rapid monitoring and management of disaster.

Apart from the IRS, ISRO is also planning the launch of seven geostationary satellites to provide very accurate information about position, velocity and time to land, marine and aerospace users. This service will be similar to the Global

Positioning System (GPS). This programme is called the Indian Regional Navigation Satellite System (IRNSS). The IRNSS satellites will function in all weathers on a 24-hour basis.

ISRO has launched many small satellites mainly for experimental purposes.

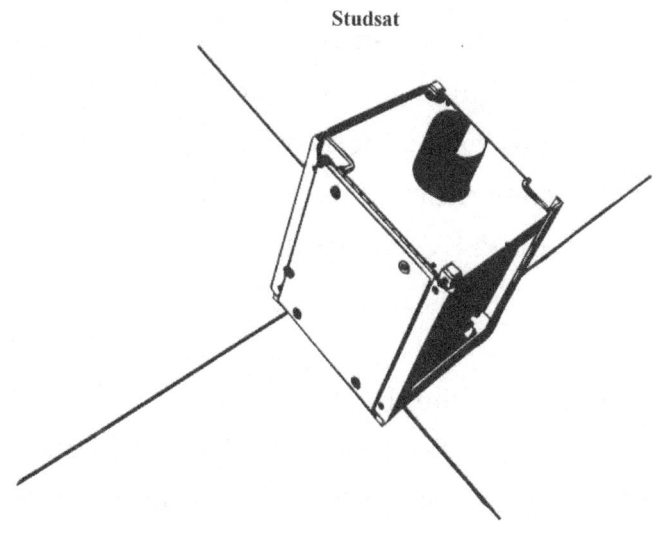

Studsat

The Student Satellite (Studsat) is a satellite developed by students of seven engineering colleges from Karnataka and Andhra Pradesh. Studsat weighs less than 1 kg. This satellite is meant for establishing a communication link between the satellite and the ground station, capturing the image of Earth and transmitting data to Earth station. Studsat was launched by PSLV on July 12, 2010.

Anusat

Anna University Satellite (Anusat) is a satellite built by students of an Indian university under the overall guidance of ISRO. The satellite demonstrates technologies relating to store and forward communications system. Anusat was launched by PSLV on April 20, 2009.

Jugnu

The nano satellite Jugnu weighing 3 kg was designed and developed by the students of Indian Institute of Technology, Kanpur, under the guidance of ISRO scientists. This satellite is intended to validate the indigenously developed camera system for imaging Earth in the near infrared region, and to evaluate the GPS receiver for its use in satellite navigation. The satellite was launched by PSLV on October 14, 2011.

SRMSat

The nano satellite SRMSat, weighing about 11 kg, was developed by the students and faculty of SRM University. This satellite addresses the problem of global warming and pollution levels in the atmosphere by monitoring carbon dioxide and water vapour. This satellite was also launched by PSLV on October 14, 2011.

SRE

ISRO successfully launched the Space-capsule Recovery Experiment (SRE) in 2007. With the launch of this satellite and its recovery, ISRO proved that it could launch a satellite in space and bring it back safely to Earth. The SRE satellite, which weighed 550 kg, was sent to orbit in space and after twelve days of orbiting, it was brought back and made to fall in the Bay of Bengal. When the frogmen of the Indian Coast Guard recovered the satellite from the sea, it was in good shape. The success of the SRE experiment has given ISRO an understanding of how orbiting satellites can re-enter Earth and how they can be recovered. Re-entry and recovery technology is a pre-requisite for manned space missions.

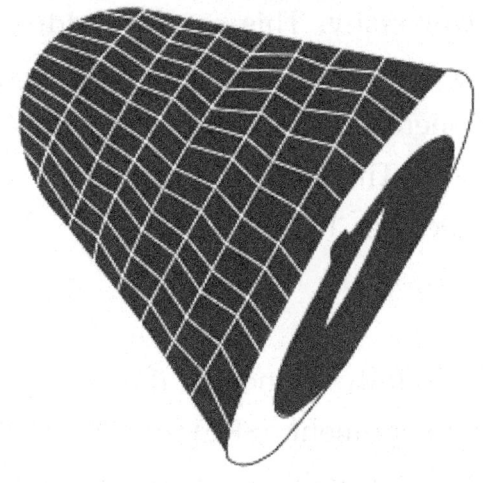

The SRE Satellite

What are the scientific satellites built by ISRO?

ISRO has built several scientific satellites including Aryabhata, SROSS-C and Megha-Tropiques.

Megha-Tropiques was launched on October 12, 2011 by a PSLV flight. This satellite, a joint venture of ISRO and the French National Space agency, is intended to study the systems that influence

SROSS-C

tropical weather and climate. The tropical belt receives more energy from the sun than it radiates back into space. The excess energy is transported to other regions by the motion of the atmosphere and oceans. The Megha-Tropiques satellite is intended to study the water cycle and energy exchanges in the tropical region.

Data from the instruments on board the Megha-Tropiques satellite enhances scientific knowledge in the field of climate research in the tropical region. Other than the scientists in India and France, there are already 21 scientific teams from Australia, Brazil, Italy, Japan, Korea, Niger, Sweden, the UK and USA using data from Megha-Tropiques.

Another scientific satellite built by ISRO is ASTROSAT. This satellite is a space-borne astronomy observatory for conducting multi-wavelength studies. Most astronomical objects in the universe emit radiation spanning the complete electromagnetic spectrum, from long wavelength radio waves to very short wavelength gamma rays. To understand the physical processes of multi-wavelength astronomy, it is essential to carry out simultaneous observations. ASTROSAT is also studying the determination of black hole masses and the linkages between micro-quasars and quasars.

What are ISRO's space exploration satellites?

Chandrayaan-1 was ISRO's first space exploration mission. It consisted of an orbiting spacecraft that housed and supported scientific instruments. It also carried a lander (Moon Impact Probe) that took off from the orbiting spacecraft and crash-landed on the surface of the moon.

The Chandrayaan-1 mission had three objectives. The first was to photograph the surface of the moon in such a way that the length, breadth and height of the surface features of the moon could be measured more accurately. The second objective was to prepare an accurate map of the moon, showing how the various elements and minerals are distributed over its surface. The third was to prepare a map of the moon that shows different geological areas clearly.

There were eleven scientific instruments (payloads) in the satellite through which the objectives of the mission were to be achieved. Of these, five instruments were designed and developed in India. One was from Bulgaria and two were from the United States. Three instruments were from the European Space Agency, one of which was developed jointly with India, and the other was with Indian contribution.

The Chandrayaan-1 spacecraft achieved all these objectives. The most important achievement of the mission was that it discovered water on the lunar surface. It was India's stepping stone into planetary exploration, and the spacecraft faced immense challenges in the harsh lunar environment. But it was a giant leap for India's space programme and led to the one of the biggest scientific discoveries of the twenty-first century.

ISRO is sending another mission to the moon, called Chandrayaan-2. This mission will have a lander and a rover. The rover will rove over the moon's surface and collect data about the environment of the moon.

The Mars Orbiter Mission (MOM) of ISRO has caught the attention of the world for its realization with a cost just one tenth of similar missions undertaken elsewhere. In addition, it also created history by being successful in its first attempt. The MOM spacecraft carries five scientific instruments, all developed indigenously in India, to provide crucial information about our neighbouring planet.

9
The Satellites of the Future

What will satellites do for us in future?

A lot has happened since Sputnik 1 went to space in October 1957. Back in 1955, the idea that satellites may serve a useful purpose was dismissed as a flight of fancy. Today, their utility is taken for granted.

Right now, more than 3,000 satellites are circling the globe. Over the years, satellites have been called upon to perform many tasks. Satellite technologies have improved and have become more complex, and space scientists have pushed the boundaries of space exploration. As a result, we have developed a much better understanding of how the laws of orbit mechanics operate and gained greater knowledge in designing, assembling and operating satellites. Today, communication satellites are many times more powerful than their predecessors. New generations of small satellites are delivering more affordable services.

Formation flying is one of the key technologies for future satellites. Formation flying is about multiple satellites flying together, working as a group on a single mission objective. This allows constellations of smaller, cost-effective satellites to offer capabilities currently available only with more expensive systems. Formation flying technologies will bring new and better quality results from all kinds of missions. Mastering formation flying depends on developing advanced technologies in areas such as meteorology and satellite guidance, navigation and control.

Space exploration is no longer a thing of the future. Chandrayaan-1 has already found water on the moon. Orbiting spacecrafts such as Mars

Odyssey and Mars Express have confirmed the existence of ice under the surface of Mars. The spacecraft New Horizons, that was launched by NASA in 2006, flew past Jupiter in 2007 and will arrive at Pluto in 2015 before it flies away to the Kuiper belt.

But although the search has only begun, there is still a long way to go. As dreamers and doers assure us, we will finally realize our dream of building human colonies on other planets in this decade. The future of the human species in the long term lies in space. Like our ancestors, who went out to new areas of the planet to survive and prosper, we have a destiny that will take us away from Earth to find new places to live.

10
Experiments

Launching a Satellite

Objective

The objective of the experiment is to find out the principle of launching a satellite into space.

The Idea

If we imagine that we have climbed a mountain whose summit is above Earth's atmosphere (it has to be an imaginary mountain because it would be about ten times higher than Mount Everest), and we throw a ball from the summit of the mountain, it would fall to the ground in a curved path. The faster we throw the ball, the farther it will go before it hits the ground. If we can throw the ball at a certain high speed, it would circle the Earth in a curved path. This is the speed needed to put satellites into orbit. We cannot throw the ball at that high a speed, but the idea of this experiment is to understand how increasing force influences distances involved.

Materials

1. A table
2. A marble
3. Chalk

Procedure

1. Roll a marble off the edge of a table
2. Get a classmate to mark with chalk where the marble leaves the table and where it first hits the floor. The curved path between the two points is its trajectory.
3. Repeat the process using greater force each

time. Measure the distance between the chalk marks on the floor which indicate where the marble lands each time.
4. Find out how did its trajectory (its curved path after it leaves the table) changed each time.

What is the scientific explanation for this?

The scientific explanation is the Newton's first law of motion. This law points out that an object at rest, such as a rocket at launch pad, needs the exertion of an unbalanced force to lift it off. The amount of force produced by the engines of the rocket has to be greater than the force of gravity that holds it down. As long as the thrust of the engines continues, the rocket will accelerate.

Sensory Remote Sensing

Objective

The objective of the experiment is to find examples of remote sensing in your everyday life.

The Idea

Remote sensing is a technique used to gather information about an object or an area without actually touching it. Our eyes, ears, and skin help us in remote sensing. These sensors provide information about size, colour, location, temperature and other conditions of an object. The idea is to learn how we practise sensory remote sensing in our daily lives.

Materials

1. Pieces of cloth
2. Paper
3. Pencils
4. Markers or crayons
5. Liquids of various scents such as of lemon, garlic or perfumes of different scents

Procedure

1. Create a smell trail around the room by soaking pieces of cloth with liquids of different scents. Place the cloth pieces around the room.

2. Draw up a map of the room showing doors, windows and any other landmark.
3. Now get a friend to locate the scents by remote sensing, i.e., by using his or her nose.
4. Get your friend to mark X's on the map to indicate the location of the scents.
5. You can assign a different colour to each scent and make a key or legend to show what scent each colour represents.

What is the significance of this exercise?

What you now have is a sensory map of the classroom. This is a good example of what remote sensing does: it gathers information about an object or area without actually touching it. We do some remote sensing almost every day. For example, smelling our breakfast or dinner being cooked, taking a photograph, feeling heat from a fire, seeing lightning strike, reading an X-ray or observing stars through a telescope.

Heat Sensors

Objective

The objective of the experiment is to learn about heat sensors of a weather satellite.

The Idea

Weather satellites make measurements of the temperature in Earth's atmosphere, record sea surface temperatures and monitor cloud cover and ice boundaries. At an altitude of about 900 km, the heat sensors of these satellites scan the entire surface of Earth over a 24-hour period, and measure the temperatures of the oceans, the land, the air and the clouds. The idea is to find out how the heat sensor works.

Materials

1. Paper
2. Pencil
3. A tray of ice
4. A bowl of hot water

Procedure

1. Place a tray of ice near a bowl of hot water

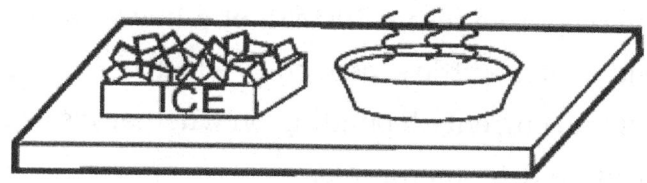

2. Move your hand over the ice, and then, over hot water. To give your temperature reading, say 'Hmm' if you do not feel any particular temperature. Say 'Brr' when you feel cold. Say 'Wow' when you feel the heat.
3. Ask your friend to draw on a paper with a pencil. He should move the pencil in the same direction as your hand is moving, making a straight solid line for 'Hmm', a zigzagged line for 'Wow', and a dotted line for 'Ber'.

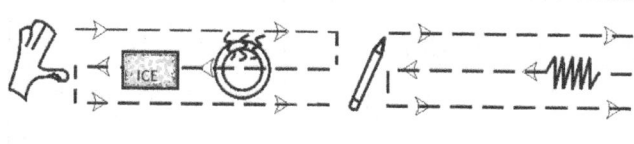

Heat Sensor Equipment

What is the significance of this experiment?

This is how a heat sensor of a satellite is designed, in very simple terms. Instead of a hand, satellite builders use a little sensor chip, which changes an electrical current, depending on whether it senses hot or cold temperatures.

A satellite detects temperature differences and sends back information to create an infrared image in black and white and shades of grey. Colour is added by the computer to accentuate temperature differences by assigning different colours to represent different temperatures. Warm areas may appear as green, cold areas as yellow. These colours do not represent the actual colours of Earth's surface. They are called false colours, because they are not the same colours that would be seen in a normal colour photograph of the area. Our eyes and conventional cameras cannot visually detect the difference between hot and cold. We rely on other senses to do that.

Made in the USA
Monee, IL
03 May 2026